NO SCALES NEEDED

A DRAGON SHIFTER FATED MATES STORY

MICHELLE ZIEGLER

Suddenly, fighting my inner demons has a whole new meaning.

I went through hell and back just to end up in a constant nightmare. Well, maybe nightmare is wrong? Going back to normal life, though, is proving to be harder than I expected.

My saving grace? A man with strange green eyes that I hallucinated turned into a dragon. It was all a hallucination, wasn't it?

How can I go back to being just a teacher when no matter what I tell myself, no matter what anyone tells me, I know the world as we see it isn't so simple? There is more, and whatever that scientist did to me has cursed me.

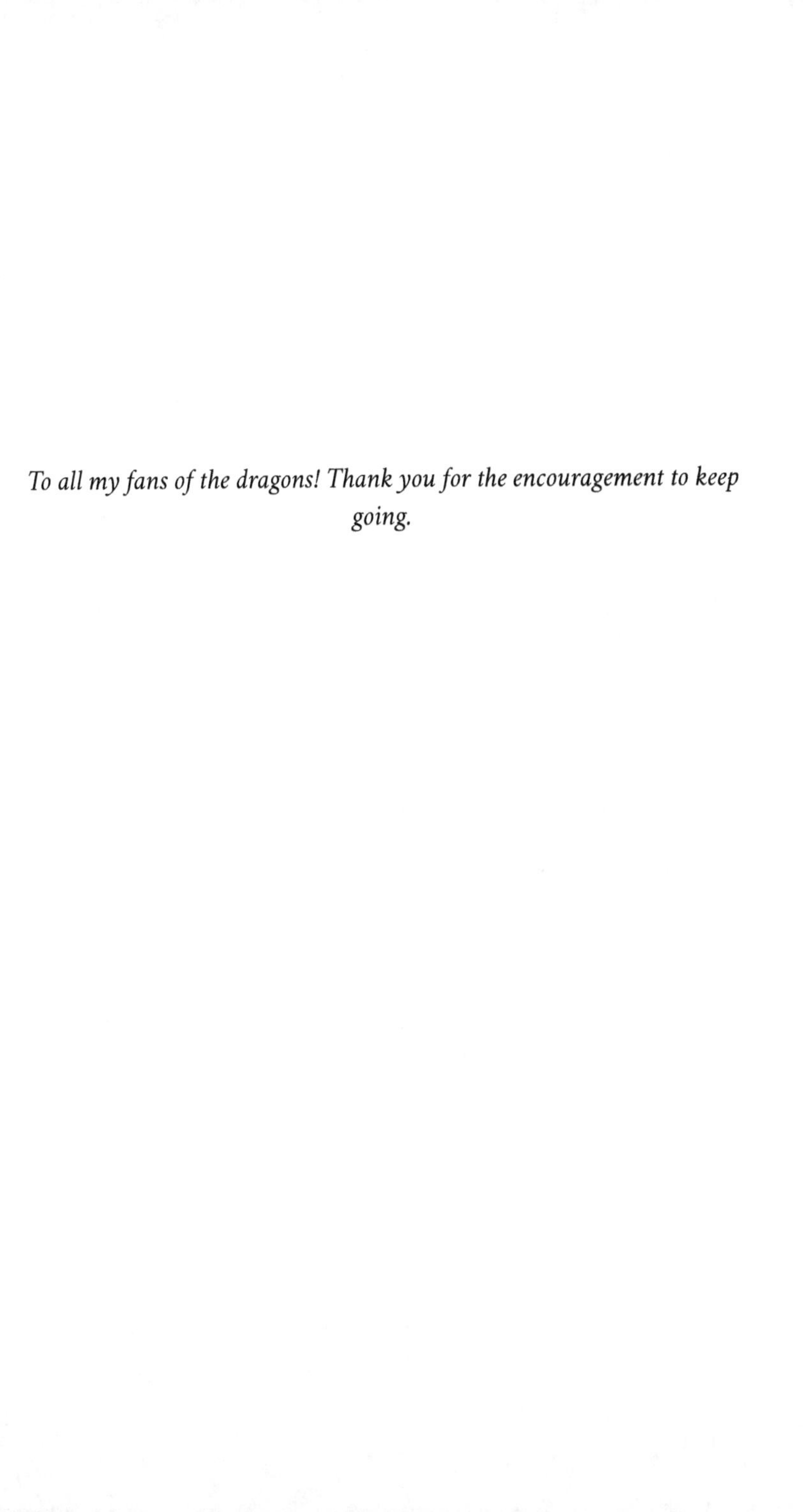

To all my fans of the dragons! Thank you for the encouragement to keep going.

ACKNOWLEDGMENTS

Life isn't easy. We are all different and those differences make us who we are. I should tell the world thank you for being you, because you inspire characters to be who they are.

My husband and kids always deserve my biggest thanks for letting me have time to get these characters out into the world!

I have so many readers to thank, but especially my Beta/Alpha readers. Thanks Lucia, Bev, Carol, and Donise! They have a knack for reading between the lines.

Thank you Emcat Designs for my cover and Editing by Elizabeth for services.

Of course, my review team is a group that has my undying gratitude!

AND ALWAYS! Thank you readers! Thank you for giving me a chance and escaping into my world and loving some confused dragon shifters from outer space. Thank you for following me this far into this crazy adventure.

ABOUT THE AUTHOR

Michelle's imagination started spilling out onto paper the second she could scribble. Her drawing never improved, but her love affair with words continued and evolved as she became infatuated with one story after another. If life could be written, Michelle would write everyone's ending as a happily ever after.

Michelle grew up in Chicago and later moved to Colorado. Her husband still makes fun of her Midwest accent. She has traded in her engineering degree to raise two little humans and three dogs, and prays she survives it all. Her sanity survives on the pages she writes. As Michelle always says, in a world of serious she writes an escape.

Website: http://www.michellezieglerauthor.com
Newsletter: http://michellezieglerauthor.com/contact/

facebook.com/MichelleZieglerAuthor
twitter.com/MZiegler_Writer
instagram.com/mziegler_writer

FOREWORD

Do you remember where the dragons are?

So far four brothers have found mates! Kal and Maddie, Edric and Lilly, Deo and Aisha, Nyke and Irene, and now... well you need to read.

Book one we met the evil doctor with his first attempt at getting to a mate and a dragon. He's bad news. Like even the Illuminati's branch of paranormal beliefs is afraid of this guy. I digress. Book two Eadric needed to Win over Lilly who was terrified of just about everything. She had a right having been locked away forever. Her connection to the doctor saved Maddie. Aisha was the last ditch effort to figure out poisons and antidotes with her magical side of things, but in the end she couldn't do what Lilly did for Maddie. That's okay though, she has other uses. Like being Deo's mate. Nyke saved Lilly from the doctor only to realize she wasn't entirely sure what to do with her freedom or where to go. She had her own demons to fight in order to accept her future as Nyke's mate.

Alright. You're caught up! I hope you're ready for this next mate. We are so close to winning this war on evil. One more piece to the puzzle and we will beat him!

The sheets clung to her skin as she bolted up. Her chest heaving in the air, Jenn tried to slow her breathing, just like the therapist had told her to. It had been a week since she'd been kidnapped, and it felt more and more real than it had that night.

"It wasn't real."

The words of the therapist swirling around in her head.

A man that turns into a dragon. Not real. That was a hallucination. Creatures that clung to walls and had glowing eyes. Not real. That's what they kept telling her. The police never found the building, although Jenn was certain she was remembering it all wrong. It existed, but she couldn't be sure where.

She was also positive that the dragon that had rescued her had been just as real. But no. None of it was real. Right?

The green dragon had seemed real, though, and so did the green eyes of her hot new rescuer. Was she making him up?

She let her head lull back on her shoulders for a minute. She could do this. Get on with life. She could put it all back to normal. The wind blew outside and something scratched at her window.

"Just a branch. Just like the last seven times. Just branches."

Her heart slowed, and finally she was able to gasp in air. This was okay. She could do this. Get back to normal. That was what she needed. She slid her sweaty body to the edge of the bed and took in another breath. Her feet slid against the cool wood of the floor and she closed her eyes.

This was fine. She had PTSD and nothing she was making up was real. The therapist said so. There were no demons. There were no ghosts. There were no dragons.

Slowly, she rose from her bed and padded to the window. Pushing aside the blinds, she peeked into the sun. Maybe it was only to confirm that the branch that tormented her was back at its taunt. The world was quiet now. Nothing strange.

Something caught her eyes, and she blinked a few times, but no. No dragon was really out there. Pulling the drapes further open, she squinted against the sun. She wasn't crazy. Probably.

The dark lines had started to fade along her arms. Jenn knew she was supposed to see the doctor, but she couldn't. Well, not the doctors they wanted her to see.

Rubbing the veins, she shook. No more needles for the rest of her life. One thing Jenn knew was real were the two men that rescued her. They were real. But they were men, not dragons.

After she'd been saved, she'd woken up to the most beautiful, chiseled features. At first, she feared he couldn't have been real. Maybe a god, but no way was he human. Except she'd felt him with her own hands. He'd taken her to the hospital, and that hadn't gone well. Jenn didn't like hospitals, but thanks to everything, she had to. She'd been kidnapped.

Jenn had to talk to the police and that forced her to not only piece together her kidnapping, but to analyze what was real and what wasn't. Although she ended up sounding insane.

Dreams or nightmares, she was free. How had he gotten her out of there, though? She knew how she got out of the pit, but how had the second guy saved her? He'd flown.

No one asked him though, and it's probably because she said he saved her. That was mostly true. He made her feel safe, and that removed him from any suspect list. But her mind knew there had been two such men and neither of them was human.

There was no hope of remembering what had happened. She tried to remember. Had she really been found on the side of a road, like the man, no Barak, said? Had she really just been wandering?

The room, the creatures, all seemed real. The burn of the injections was real. She had the lines to prove that they were real.

She'd had to fight the police and the doctors. Thankfully, they wouldn't or didn't push her. No, everyone was worried he was going to break. And maybe she was.

It had been so real. She held her arms close to her body, hugging herself, shaking.

The dreams were getting worse. Every night, it was the same. She could sense something else out there and as much as she wanted to believe that this was all made up, the man, Deo and his friend Barak told her none of this was made up.

But they'd told the police they'd found her.

Slowly, she stepped away from the window. She needed to shower and change her sheets again. She needed to put on real clothes, ones that didn't have an elastic waist or stains. She needed to get back to her students.

Blowing out a breath, she decided to move in a forward direction. The shower direction.

Turning the knob, she let the water steam up the room as she leaned against the sink. The room turned into a foggy filled dream.

Something inside her awakened as she relaxed into the heat.

The visions from her sleep came alive in front of her. Replaying. Last night she dreamt of a woman. Not in a sexual way, but in a badass way. She was saving the world from the creatures that haunted Jenn.

Without thinking, Jenn reached for the images and grabbed air.

There was nothing to touch or grab. No one there to vanquish the demons.

Blinking away the vision, she remembered where she was. Ready to shower. Right.

Peeling off the tank top and underwear that were saturated with another night of restless sleeping, she dropped them on the floor. The mirror met her gaze, foggy glass blocking her from seeing the new and not so improved her.

Even she could feel the difference in her body. She'd wanted to go on a diet for years. It just never seemed like a good time.

Strange drugs might not have been the original plan, but they seemed to reduce her to half of what she once was, and she missed her curves. The healthy curves of a woman who, for the most part, had loved who she was.

Jenn scratched at her forearms again, subconsciously. No. She didn't have use for a mirror anymore. Not to remind her that regardless of what the therapist said or the police report said, it had all been real.

She pulled aside the curtain and peeked in. Making sure nothing changed in the last twenty seconds. It was like she expected something to pop out and say "Zuul" and haunt her shower. Anything was possible, regardless of what she was trying to tell herself.

She started to get in and paused. No. First, she needed to lock the bathroom door. Then she would shower. Maybe she should just take off the curtain? Yeah. She should just get rid of the curtain. Fix the issue of someone surprising her.

She hesitated, pulling her hand away and then darting it back. Slowly, she pulled the hooks off the shower bar and gently folded the fabric and set it down next to the tub. The spray of the shower posed a new issue. One, her sanity cared so much less about.

All this just to take a shower. Damn, her life sucked.

"They aren't real. Nothing is real."

Was nothing truly real?

Pursing her lips, she looked around.

Nope. Water was real, and it was going to ruin her crappy faux wood floors. She grabbed up the folded curtain and stretched it across the floor, pressing it close to the tub. There, that would work. Or something. She still felt better about it. She couldn't do another speed shower. She needed to try and figure out how to deal with living in a constant scary place that no one else could see.

Finally, she stepped in and let the heat of the water sink into her body. She tried not to replay the visions, but something felt strange.

Grabbing up shampoo, she tried to keep one eye open this time instead of both. She could live without vision in one, but both? Well, soap really hurt when you got it in both eyes.

A shiver ran up her spine and she started rinsing the shampoo out before she was even sure she'd washed her hair. But she could shake the paranoia.

A girl in her dreams haunted her. She couldn't shake a strange feeling, like she knew her. Or well, knew she existed and something was pulling her to find her. That seemed absurd, though.

Right?

How was she supposed to go back to a normal life with everything she'd seen? How was she supposed to forget that an entire world she'd never known about existed and no one believed her?

Well, except for someone did. Two someones. One with strange green eyes. Barak. The dragon she'd ridden. Although she hadn't seen him shift since that night, she swore that he had been real. He'd carried her away from the nightmare.

The guy, Deo. He'd been real. He'd been a dragon, and he'd gotten her out of that dungeon.

But had she made that up?

No. The men were very real. Barak's mere presence did something to her every time he showed up.

She hadn't been able to bring herself to ask if there was more to them than what she could see. Just knowing how big they were, much larger than any man she'd ever dated, there had to be.

Water ran down her body, and she let it run over her face, trying to wash away the panic that never seemed too far from the surface. If she asked them and they shifted into winged beasts, she would have to face the fact whatever she knew about the world was wrong. Or at least incomplete.

Running her fingers through her hair, she tried to hang on to the familiar. She could do this. Keep her cool. Keep her sanity. But, really, she was numb. Nothing felt the same.

How could she go on teaching her seventh-graders world history and wondering the entire time if what she taught them was real or if there had been more to the story? Were there other creatures involved? Something humans didn't know about that ended World War II or perhaps maybe started one crisis or another?

Something crashed on the other side of the bathroom door, and she froze. Her entire body felt like every inch of it was alive in panic. She needed a weapon. She grabbed for whatever was to her right as the door crashed open.

"What the fuck?" yelled a now familiar voice. Barak.

He paused. She paused. His eyes wandered over her wet body.

She shivered under the scrutiny. It took her a second to come to her senses before she screamed at him, but not before feeling something strange and hungry awaken within her.

Apparently, she wasn't entirely numb, not anymore.

"Get out. What do you think you're doing? You just broke down my door," she screamed.

He smiled. "And you are about to attack me with a - what is that?

She looked at the thing in her hands. "Uh. A pumice stone on a stick?"

He smirked. "Are you sure of this, pumice, on a stick?"

It took several seconds for her brain to catch up with what was happening and then Jenn proceeded to freak out. She didn't have enough damn hands to cover her breasts, her nether regions, and hold her useless weapon. She sure as hell was going to try to do it all, though.

"What are you doing in my bathroom? Turn around," she screeched.

Jenn swore his eyes flickered between something human and something else. The green of his irises swirling like an unearthly aurora.

"As you wish."

She glared at him, only he didn't seem to notice. She stuck her tongue out.

"I can hear you moving and from the sounds of it, you opened your mouth. Does it need to be put to better use than yelling at me?" he asked.

Her cheeks heated.

"No. No, my mouth is fine. You don't have to guard the bathroom door. I was just showering."

He didn't move and even if he was turned around; it didn't stop whatever this new and welcome feeling was. She swore that she could see every muscle of his back under the cotton of his shirt. What was the point of shirts when men had muscles like that.

"Can you at least try to shut the door and then I will yell at you once I get out?" she asked. Reluctance seemed to lace every word. If he was here, nothing could hurt her. He was what made her feel safe. Logic didn't help her understand why.

She was mesmerized by the muscles in his neck as he shook his head.

"No, I will not be closing you off ever again. You didn't answer the door. You had me concerned. I will not be letting you out of my sight."

"You're not even looking at me for me to be in your sight."

He shrugged. "You think I only have one sense to know you're close. Continue your shower and I will guard you. Next time you will be answering your door."

She smirked. "Right. That's what you think."

This time he did glance over his shoulder, and she scrambled to cover up again.

"Princess, I can play this game for as long as you like."

2

My pants were my least favorite human invention. Jenn, even in her fearful and abused state, was gorgeous. Jenn naked and wet?

His dick twitched.

Perfect. He licked his lips, imagining what she would taste like as she came for him. Only, he wasn't going to get that pleasure for some time.

This was definitely slow. His mate seemed to be confused. Confused and suffering and he struggled with how to help her.

Right now, though, he enjoyed the look in her eyes as she watched him appreciate everything about her. She wasn't healthy yet, but Deo was helping with that. And that there had been the issue. This was the first time she'd actually looked at him, instead of Deo.

He'd had to overcome the jealousy. Deo swore it was simply the fact he'd been the one to pull her out of that hell. Barak couldn't convince himself that it was anything except she obviously wanted Deo. She'd never given him that impression, though. It was that she never looked at him and it killed him. It killed his dragon. They wanted their mate to see them.

"Are you done yet?"

He knew she wasn't. He could hear the splash of the water. Hell, the droplets changed pitch as they ran over her body. But he wanted to hear her voice. Hear the sweet sound as she talked to him. This had to be a good sign. Something changing. Her eyes held life.

The first couple of days had not only scared him as she'd looked on into nothing, but the fact she didn't know him. No reaction. His dragon struggled to give her space. Barak's hands itched to touch her. But she suffered and he was apparently the last thing she wanted.

Her voice perked his ears.

"Seriously? You barge into my bathroom, probably broke some locks and scare me half to death and you want to know if I'm done?"

The soft lilt of her words strummed a cord inside me.

"I could come help. You know, for any hard to reach spots," he said. He knew he needed to wait for her to come to him, but it didn't mean he didn't want to try.

He heard her hiccup her next breath and then the water turned off. Barak turned a few seconds too fast, knowing damn well she hadn't wrapped herself up yet.

"Damn it. God, can you just give me a second?

"No, and my name is Barak. Not this God you talk of. But, would you like help reaching this?"

He grabbed up the towel and held it out to her by a finger as she tried and failed to cover her delicious bits.

"Please. I'm naked. Have some decency."

He shrugged. "I don't see this as an issue? Would you prefer it if I was also naked?"

He knew the answer, but he damn well planned to try, anyway. His dick was struggling to stay calm. Barak had waited so fucking long for his mate and then to find her sick and injured, had hurt his soul. He wanted to fix her, but the wounds were deeper than anything he knew how to fix in one night or even one week.

Seeing her up and somewhat functioning seemed like a beautiful miracle from the goddess herself.

"Seriously?"

He nodded. "I am always serious."

She glared.

"Seriously?"

He nodded again. Was this a game, or did she want an answer?

"I am unsure if you are serious. You seem to like this word, though. So, yes. I am serious. I would seriously strip to make you more comfortable."

Her jaw dropped.

"I. More comfortable?"

The flush of her skin told him that his words were doing something different. Not comfort. He did enjoy the way her breasts seemed to tighten and her nipples begged to be sucked. He enjoyed the way she squirmed and grabbed for the towel.

"You're nothing like Deo, are you?"

He turned to see his brother standing in the other room, waiting to administer the antibiotics they had. Irene and Aisha still weren't entirely sure of everything that had been injected into her. All we could do was try to treat symptoms, but from the sounds of things, she was still having side effects or affects from whatever the asshole had done. Still, we would administer this round and hope for improvement.

"Much different. All of us are our own male. Is that good or bad?" he asked against the frustration of his brothers name being on her lips.

Barak looked back at the towel as it was dragged off his finger.

"I haven't decided yet," she said.

He turned his gaze back to her, disappointed as she wrapped

the towel and tucked in the corner. It didn't appear very secure. The idea of it falling in front of Deo had him struggling to contain a growl. He squeezed his fists tight. Barak already struggled with the fact that that bastard of an evil doctor thought he could force her to mate with his brother. Even if Deo had wanted none of it.

Fuck. And then there was the irrational anger that his brother had been the one to save her. Barak hadn't even known about her, yet. Fate was a bitch. The goddess had done nothing but treat her chosen warriors like fucking chess pieces. When in the hell would they be in the checkmate situation instead of pawns. He was sick of this.

She cleared her throat.

"Can I have a minute?"

The wood floor creaked as he stepped back.

"Yes. As long as you don't take too long. I can't protect you behind a closed door."

His words seemed to register, and she looked at the door and then at the splintered frame.

"I'll fix that. Sorry. I, well. I panicked. Too many things keep happening and nothing is getting better. When you didn't answer-" he stopped.

She groaned.

"Does my front door look like this too?"

Barak turned his eyes to the ceiling and ran his hands through his hair.

"I - yeah. It might."

She rolled her eyes and started to close the bathroom door. His heart rate kicked up, and he was surprised she couldn't see the damn thing beating out of his chest. He finally sucked in a breath. She pushed the door forward, and he lost sight of her, but when she stopped, the door remained ajar. He could be okay with that. Not that it would have latched in its current state, anyway. It made him feel better knowing he could at least see the movement of her at the sink.

His dick was disappointed that Barak couldn't see much more than a side view of a centimeter thin glimpse. Fine. He was hard up for her. For thinking he'd never find her to realizing that he could have lost her before he'd even had the ability to protect her. He left her and had taken to sleeping like a dog on her lawn at night.

Yeah. He was a classy stalker. The worst part, though? He could hear her tossing and turning, and he didn't know what to do about it. She never mentioned it the next day, but he'd reported it to Deo and Aisha and Irene. They'd tried something new with the medicine today, so he guessed they would see if this was a better cocktail.

He hated to see her suffering and the dark circles under her eyes said she was at the very least not sleeping. Not that he was sleeping. Maybe if they slept together?

He leaned a forearm against the bit of doorframe not resembling a splintered pincushion and leaned his forehead against his arm.

That wasn't going to happen.

"You still okay in there?" he asked. His mood had changed from playful to whatever this was. Worried? Frightened? Concerned? All of it. This planet sucked.

"Yeah. I." He could hear her swallow before she finished. "I need to go to work today."

He looked around for the source of the banging thudding away in my ears. Fuck. It was his own heart.

"What? No. You aren't ready," he finally said.

Hell, he wasn't ready.

She peeked out of the door. He could make out fabric on her shoulders. She was getting dressed and he couldn't even be reasonable enough to protest this. Loss of her naked body aside, he was worried.

"I need to be. It's been over a week and my kids need me. The therapist suggested getting back to life could help my anxiety, too. You know. Realize that what happened was a fluke."

He leaned in and pressed his palm against the door. She fought him for a second before backing away from the thing.

"A fluke? A demonic doctor tried to breed you with one of my kind. He injected you with goddess knows what and its a fluke?"

He reached a hand behind her as she backed into the wall and stopped.

"A fluke is tripping on a crack in the sidewalk or chipping a tooth on a fork. You are targeted. You have been marked and not just by that monster."

He dipped his head closer to her, pulling in her scent. His dick hardened beneath his now uncomfortable pants.

"No. Not a fluke. You are destined for - " he broke off. Did he finish his thought and tell her? Tell her she was his? He'd seen his brothers and all their mistakes. Human women didn't expect this. They didn't mate as they did, and it never seemed to be simple. Except he needed to say it.

"Me. Destined to be by my side."

She swallowed. "Maybe," she said on a breath.

Maybe? Barak pulled away, but only enough to study her face. That was unexpected. He wanted an enthusiastic yes but expected a much more violent no. Instead he got, maybe.

"Maybe," he asked.

The nod was so subtle he almost missed it. "Yeah. I don't. Well, I can't exactly say that anything isn't possible."

A slow nod seemed to have taken control of his head. Maybe. He could do maybe.

"Anything is possible," he said.

He inched in closer. He wanted to taste her. Dare he?

The beat of her heart confused him. Excited? Confused? He couldn't tell. The scent of her changed though and her eyes dilated. He stopped.

"Jenn? Are you okay?"

She didn't say anything for a second, but he could tell she wasn't seeing him. She blinked and then met his gaze.

"Where did you go?"

Her lower lip quivered.

"I don't know. I don't know anything anymore."

He leaned his forehead against hers and cradled her in his arms.

"I will kill him. I promise you that."

She nodded as a tear slid down her beautiful cheek.

"I will help you." She forced a watery laugh.

He shook his head. "No. He is all mine. I promise you though that he will die slowly and painfully if it is the last thing I ever do here."

Her eyes darted from the ceiling to the wall, and finally met his.

"Promise?"

He chuckled, but the sound wasn't light or joking.

"I promise. Princess, you will not recognize him after I make him pay for touching you."

On a false bit of confidence, he kissed her temple. She didn't pull away.

"I can promise you that I will make sure that his own mother wouldn't recognize him once I am done. I will make him cry for every soul he's ever hurt. But, he will pay for your pain first."

He kissed the top of her cheek and pulled away. He wanted to see her. Wanted to know if this was okay. If she was okay.

He would make her be okay if it was the last vow he ever made. He would protect her. Worship her and avenge her pain.

"Barak? I think it's time to let me go now."

He blinked, but moved aside.

"Never. I will never let you go."

He did however release her. Letting her do what she felt she had to. She paused and looked back over her shoulder before rounding the corner of the bathroom. The longing in her eyes was just as unexpected as the maybe. Nothing was what it seemed.

Nothing.

They needed off of this planet. But he needed her more.

3

*S*he'd made it. She was almost done.

The morning could have gone worse. Her students were happy to have her back, and getting back into a routine seemed natural. It was nice to sit at her desk. It was nice to flip through her planner. It also was eye opening to realize the world wouldn't end without her.

Somehow she'd assumed that because her life had felt like it was ending that maybe the entirety of reality ceased without her.

It did not. In fact, from what it sounded like, they'd marched on without her just fine. Minor inconveniences.

She shouldn't be distracted, but the only thing getting her through the morning was the memory of Barak's warm arms around her. He had made her feel like she mattered. Would his world end without her?

She had no family. She lived for being a teacher. But, work like anything else in the world, didn't seem to know that.

Barak though? His touch felt like life. He was oddly comforting for being an unnaturally massive man. For an unnaturally good looking man. Maybe, in between, the nightmares might have been him, haunting her dreams in a very different manner.

What she had done exactly to catch his attention was beyond her? No, that wasn't true. She'd gone and been kidnapped. Oh, and injected with some fancy drugs that screwed with her head. Seemed all worth it. Not.

"Ms. J, when is the quiz again?"

She blinked. Right. Working.

"Tomorrow. The quiz is tomorrow. Your substitute left a note that reassured me that you were all darling angels and should have no problems staying on track. Right?"

The class moaned.

"What kind of vacation did you go on?" asked one student.

She shrugged. "That's for me to know and you to never find out."

Another student raised her hand.

"My mom said you weren't on vacation but had to go to rehab."

Jenn was taken aback.

"Your mom is grossly undereducated on this matter. I was not in a rehab center."

Jenn tugged at the sleeves of her cardigan that hid the strange marks those drugs had left as a memento. No need to feed the rumors. Deo was trying to help them fade, but it was hard when no one seemed to know exactly what had been put into her veins.

"We missed you."

She smiled. "You're getting an A for that comment."

Okay, she couldn't play favorites. But really. That kid was getting an A for not making her feel like an even bigger disappointment.

Maybe she should take Deo and Barak up on their offer. Meeting their wives or, well, mates. Mates? The niggling of the truth played in her subconscious. They'd said mates. But dragons weren't real.

She took a deep breath. They'd said mates. Deo had said mate. And then? He'd shifted into a dragon. She knew he had. The words of her therapist telling her it had been the drugs filtered in. The police report said it too. Jenn's principal knew the truth of what had happened. Sort of. She wasn't about to tell her that she now believed there were demons and dragons in the world. The question was, was Jenn starting to believe herself? That she'd actually seen all of that. No one except for her seemed to question what was real.

The tightness in her chest tried to push in. No. She wasn't about to let this ruin her day. She wasn't going to let one incident define her. Too bad that one incident could.

She practiced breathing. Slow, steady breaths. She was going to be fine. It was fine. She was fine. Breathing in and out slowly, reality came into focus. Yes. She was fine. She was going to be fine.

Whatever. Maybe she wouldn't be. Why not just drive a nail into her coffin of sanity and actually just ask them if they really were dragons?

She snorted, and the class seemed to notice.

"What's so funny?"

She smiled. Funny was so not the word she was looking for. But she couldn't admit that to a class of children that still had no idea the world could be even uglier than what their parents' worst nightmares could conjure up.

"Nothing. Or well, I suppose it's just funny how everyone has a theory on where I went even when I keep saying it was a bit of a family emergency and a little vacation rolled into one."

They didn't question her. Her kids trusted, still. They needed to trust. She hoped they could trust the world was what they saw for as long as possible. Because the day they didn't trust what they saw, they would be where she was.

Waking up and wanting to hide under the covers.

They didn't need her world. The one where her darkest dreams could actually come for her.

God. Was she really contemplating they turned into dragons?

Hell. Was she really lying to her class? Yes. Yes, she was. The police report was right enough and her boss knew most of what had happened to keep her job, but right now? She was going to lie through her teeth to not destroy every little developing mind in this room.

"Alright. Let's do some quiet reading time. Better yet. Let's do some quiet reading time in the outdoor classroom."

Moans turned to little squeals of joy. She needed to get out of the classroom. Her arms itched. Her head felt warm. She just needed outside.

One by one, the kids lined up.

"Alright, Noah, you lead the way out. Thank you. Hey, all hands to ourselves friends."

The line filed out and she tried to focus, but the pain behind her eyes intensified. It was happening. She was going to get another nightmare? Daymare? What did one call trauma that just wouldn't stop?

She focused on the last kid in line.

Blond hair. Stripes. She had stripes on her shirt.

Hyper focus on the reality in front of her. That was all she could think of to get through the day. Get through her life.

One foot in front of the other.

Stripes.

She stared at a small stain on her shirt. Was it a pen? Marker? She could do this. She could not think. The stupid nightmares would go away. They would. There was no reason why they wouldn't. Deo said it was probably the trauma. PTSD.

Finally, the fresh air of outside greeted her like the first breath she'd taken from that nightmare world. She sucked in a deep breath and could feel it. The fresh air helped stave off the panic.

She was okay. She swallowed as her skin crawled.

She itched at it again and again. Focus on the fresh air. Focus on the now. Stripes. Her student had stripes. Green. The grass was green. Her throat wasn't closing up. She was fine.

"Alright kids. Find a quiet spot and hunker down. Enjoy the fresh air."

Everyone did as told, giving her another few seconds of quiet to gather herself.

Things had been fine for the first part of the day until they weren't.

Why now? She couldn't figure it out.

Something shadowy and dark wafted around the air. Slithering. She looked around to see if any of the kids could see it. Nothing. She was certain they didn't because mass hysteria did not ensue. It's not real.

None of it is real. Dragons aren't real. Demons aren't real. It's not real.

It was though. It was real, and she wasn't fine.

She needed to leave. She'd come back too soon. It was her fault. She shouldn't be here.

The world was collapsing in on her. She could feel it. She could feel her chest tighten and it was harder and harder to breath.

What could she do?

"Jenn? I found you."

She spun around at a voice that was out of place.

"Barak?"

His too perfect smile was all she could see as the sun blinded her and a flood of calm washed over me.

"Yes. I'm official. See." He lifted the corner of his shirt.

"What? What am I looking at?"

He stopped an inch from her, and she breathed in his odd spicy scent that enhanced her calm. She wanted more of that. Ever since that hellish place. Ever since he'd help rescue her, she could catch his scent like a damn blood hound. The thing was, right now, she didn't mind. She needed him.

She blinked as he cleared his throat and whispered. "You okay?"

Jenn shook her head and tried to hide the quiver in her lip.

"Thought so. Well, you are looking at a fully background checked mental health volunteer."

She looked at him. "Thats not a thing."

The heat of his fingers brushed her cheek as he brushed her hair aside.

"Actually, a volunteer is a volunteer and after talking to your principal I showed her my very impressive background in PTSD counseling. She has allowed me to observe your classroom while I work on my degree."

She blinked. "Degree?"

He shrugged. "Come to dinner with me and I'll explain everything?"

The shuffling behind her told her that her students weren't reading.

"Get back to reading you nosy small humans."

They giggled, and she turned back to them.

"Are you going to have dinner with the nice man, Miss J?"

Barak kept his distance, but she could still feel the heat of him. She could still feel him there and all she wanted to do was sink into the comfort that was him.

"Why would I go to dinner with someone who just crashed our outdoor reading session?"

She crossed her arms over her chest and popped her hip. Instead of anyone taking her serious the kids laughed.

"So? You saying yes to the pretty man?" another girl asked.

She rolled her eyes and noticed all the girls were all starry-eyed. Damn it all to hell.

"Fine. But also, he said he is here to volunteer in the classroom. So maybe we should put him to work?"

Oddly, the boys were the ones jumping up first.

"Sweet. Is he like a football guy? Are we doing football?"

One of the other boys starting walking around him. Maybe sizing him up? She held in a laugh.

"Nah. He doesn't do football. What do you do? You some kind of spy? You look like you could kill someone with your finger."

Her jaw dropped. "Jacob, no. You go finish silent reading. We will treat Mr.-" she paused.

"What should the kids call you?"

He smiled as he leaned into her. "Yours?"

The kids didn't hear him, but she sure did. Her entire body warmed and all too quickly, he was moving in front of her.

"Call me Mr. B, since you call your teacher Miss. J. Seems fitting? Don't you agree? So what are we reading?"

And then as she watched him fold his massive body onto a small stump next to one of the boys, one of the boys that oddly was one of more quiet ones, her heart melted. It's like he knew what kid could use some added confidence. It's like he knew who she would have loved to reach more. It's like he knew her.

4

He could handle kids. There didn't exactly seem to be a ton back home. Not in the dragon parts of the world, anyway. Finding soul mates was a pain in the ass. Once they found them, though, breeding was important. It's just there weren't exactly millions of dragon warriors. Still, he liked kids. He would like kids for her.

He would like anything this woman liked, and right now, she liked her job.

He'd caught the scent of fear though the second he'd come out of the building. She might have looked put together and ready to take on the world, but her pulse and her scent told him he'd been right to find a way to help her. He'd been right to come for her.

Barak glanced up from his spot on the ground and sought out his future mate. She sat next to one of her students and he listened to the rhythm of her heart. Calmer now. Something inside him calmed, and the dragon curled up in wait for her. He'd given her peace, or he hoped he had. A smile met her as she glanced his way. Her cheeks colored pink as he met her eyes, and she quickly looked away.

He'd have to thank his brothers later. Hacking a few systems and a few hours invested into the day and he was not only FBI approved, he was a senior at Aisha's college in some psychology program. Whatever. It got his approval here. The principal took one look at his letter of recommendations from whoever Aisha had blackmailed and here he was. Student teaching or some such bullshit.

Really, what he needed to do was stay close to her and, from the sight of her panicking, he was almost too late. Fast as they'd worked, it still took up nearly an entire week to come up with a plan to watch her while also trying to figure out how to stop the evil asshole that was ruining lives left and right. It had nearly ruined everything; her going back to work already.

Somehow, the goddess blessed him, though, and it all fell in line. He was here before she melted down. Now the question was, how much did this place really mean to her? He needed her. But his need would take her light years away.

"Alright, kids. Let's head back in. School's almost done for the day."

The girl he'd sat near giggled as she got up. "You're here to help, Miss. J forever?"

Help? Forever? He so wanted to answer the way he wanted to. The way his damn dragon wanted to. The dragon stretched inside him and he had to strain against his need to break free.

"Sure. Or for as long as she'll need me. Now, get in line."

He winked at the student and it seemed to get a lot of giggles, but she was in line and walking in.

Jenn seemed to be keeping up with the middle of the line. At least having her out of reach made it possible to calm his soul. For a few seconds. This was not a place to get all territorial.

As they filed into the classroom, he took in the windows. The single door. Mapped out the exits. The ceiling? Possibly. He could feel the knife strapped to his calf. He would protect this woman with his life.

He couldn't leave her unprotected. So he would now sit in this classroom for as long as it took to win her.

He would do whatever it took to win her.

The kids seemed to be on autopilot? Very well trained. He slid to the back of the room and watched everything happen. Backpacks were grabbed from the floor or hooks over on the wall.

"Great. While we wait for the bell, please check your planners. No excuses for being late on assignments just because I had to be away."

He raised a brow at her. Away? He wondered how this would all play out. The principal had been leery at first when he told her that he and Jenn had this prearranged. A few minutes into talking and she was spilling the kidnapping mess and how they were keeping it quiet from the rest of the teachers. The truth serum had worked far better than he'd expected.

Would its side effect work as well? In a few hours he hoped that the principal would remember nearly nothing of their encounter. Only that he was there and approved.

He watched Jenn's beautiful body move as she went about getting the kids ready to leave. He needed to protect her. Keep her safe. He still wished he knew what had made her a target? He supposed psychopaths didn't need reasons. Did they?

Here he would remain, at least. By her side. Pretending like he knew what he was doing. At least fear didn't scent the air anymore, and he hoped that was in largely thanks to him. Strange world, this all was. So now he knew what the school knew.

This school system was much easier to work through than the police department. Granted, they were still sniffing along the wrong roads. Jenn couldn't lead them back to the warehouses, and it was for the best. They monitored all the known locations of the good doctor and needed to keep humans away from him until they knew how to beat him.

"Are you okay?" asked Jenn.

An air of peace swept over his entire body as he looked up and smiled her way.

"I am now. You?"

He'd never noticed how she furrowed her brow when she was nervous. He could catch a whiff of the nerves, but why was she nervous around him? He'd never pushed her and he never would.

"You're too smooth, aren't you? Like you're one of those guys who knows how good he looks."

He shrugged and stepped away from the counter he was leaning on.

"Do you think I'm good looking?"

He almost missed the shudder of breath, but damn, he did like the way her eyes seemed to glisten with need?

He needed to be patient, but that wasn't easy and truthfully, he would accept her anytime she was ready. Anytime. He sniffed again and let the scent of her fill him with every feeling she inspired. It didn't, however, do his pants or his dick any favors.

"You know I and every female on the planet think you are." She paused, and he was about to speak when she said something unexpected. "And so is Deo. Are the rest of the brothers you talk about the same?"

The muscle in his temple twitched, and he was pretty sure that his eyes nearly popped from his face.

"Why are we talking of them? They are of no concern to you."

She smiled.

"Well, to be fair, Deo did rescue me. I'll probably always have respect for him. And anyway, we were just talking about who I thought was hot. Sure. You're good looking, but so is he."

His dragon freaked the fuck out, and his skin shifted between scales back to human. He knew she'd noticed by the way she stepped back, stopping as she knocked into a desk.

"What is that?"

He spoke through clenched teeth. "My dragon doesn't like you noticing Deo, or any other male for that matter."

She made a strange little hmph noise. He narrowed his eyes.

"Interesting. Your dragon. Is that what we call them these days?"

He stepped towards her. She backpedaled quickly and nearly fell again.

Wrapping his arm around her, his hand splayed across her back. He could feel the spike in her body heat.

"Tell me, what do you think? Do you think I am calling anything a dragon other than the very creature that burns in my soul for you? I don't know what else you refer to. But my dragon, my soul, my heart burn bright for no one but you, Jenn."

Her breath came out in a rush. He could imagine kissing her. And maybe he should try. Because waiting sucks.

"I. I don't know what you are talking about."

The wavering in her voice had his mind filling with questions. He'd expected her to react to the dragon differently. Freak out he would shift indoors? That seemed logical. To question what his dragon was, though? Confusing. Very confusing. His best ability to help her would be to mate her and understand her mind. But that wasn't an option. Instead, he listened to her heart pitter patter away. Not scared. Aroused? Maybe? He sniffed the air. It was a confused mess. And that's when it hit him. She was hiding from him. Not physically, but emotionally. Something wasn't as it seemed.

"What do you want to know? There is something you aren't asking me."

She blew out a breath and wiggled out of his grasp a little. The curves of her body under his fingers as he held her tight left little to his imagination. It would be easy to pull her against him, against his already aching hard on. He couldn't do that, though. All the same, he wasn't letting go, not until he was ready to let her go.

She was supposed to be here, in his arms. He was made to love her and only her for now, until the day he drew in his last breath. Wars were fought and won, but he'd never seen how hard the emotional battles were. Impossible.

"You can tell me. Ask me anything. Even without you knowing. Without a single promise from your lips, I am already bound to you. I would no more leave you than I could my brothers. I am yours, Jenn." His throat mirrored sandpaper as he swallowed. He reached to push a bit of hair back behind her ear, but he hesitated. She didn't flinch. "I am yours, now until my very last breath and even then my soul would go on loving you until we are united again."

Her heart sped up. Her body temperature rose. She trembled. He didn't want her afraid of him and he didn't want to admit that perhaps he was more afraid of losing her than he'd realized.

"Anything you want to know, I will answer." Was losing her an option? Fuck, this was hard. Running his hand over her arm, he tried for reassuring again and again. The connection calmed his fears a little. She remained there, allowing him to connect them through touch. He pushed the sleeve of the sweater higher to give him more skin, kissing the veins of poison with his fingertips. He couldn't erase this past for her, no matter what his soul desired.

"Jenn, you must talk to me. I can't remove your pain, but I can help you. Use me. Rely on me."

She took a deep breath and the idea that she might finally talk to him soothed a hole deep inside him.

"Are you a real dragon?"

Tipping her chin with his fingers, he narrowed his gaze. Odd question, he thought. Nothing in her rounded eyes or serious set of her mouth told him that this was a joke. He waited to see if she cracked a smile. Was she playing with him?

The muscles at her temples twitched, and he slid his thumb over her jawline, feeling the tension settling in. No, she was most definitely not joking.

The sour taste of worry settled into the back of his throat. She didn't know him. Everything he'd done had been under the assumption she'd known him. But somehow that wasn't the case.

The memory of pulling her out of that hell of creatures was clear as the morning's breakfast to him. He'd been wrong to assume he'd made an impression on her or that she would remember him as well.

There was nothing to do but to answer her.

Start over from the beginning with her.

Show her what she obviously didn't remember.

5

"Yes. I'm real. My dragon is real."

He tilted his head, and she shrunk into herself.

She couldn't say anything. This had been what she wanted to know. But now she couldn't shake the fear. If he was real then she wasn't crazy and if he wasn't, well. She wanted him to be real. A real dragon? She didn't care, really. She just wanted Barak to be the hero she needed. The one that she swore she dreamt had swept her away. A dream. Unlike the rest of the nightmares. The visions of him brought her joy, and she preferred them the most. Too bad she couldn't choose what she dreamt of all the time.

"You've seen me," Barak continued.

She blinked away her panic.

This had been what she'd feared. Not only an answer to say the glimpses were real, but that he would judge her.

He slowly released her as she fought against the noodles she called legs. His hesitation told her he wasn't entirely sure if she was stable or not. He seemed almost afraid to let her go. She didn't want him to see her differently, though. One more fear to add to her growing bonfire of feelings that she was trying to overcome. Instead, they seemed to all burn together, creating the worst cocktail of suffocating smoke that she couldn't sift through. She couldn't determine how she felt from one second to the next.

A dragon. A real dragon.

She held her breath. Could he see her plea to not give up on her? She blinked away whatever feelings were trying to surface. No. She could push it all aside.

"Yes. I mean, I can't remember much. Everything seems like a haze. Those drugs were awful."

She broke off. A rancid taste filled the back of her mouth the second she spoke of the memories. A memory that she could still manifest. She could still remember the aftertaste of one of the injections. Or maybe that had been some gas? She couldn't even trust herself to know what she remembered. Everything was too weird to be real. But then there were these guys. They were real. They were here. He was here. Which means everything she remembered had to be real.

Barak gripped her wrist and pushed up the sleeves of the sweater she wore. She was trying to cover the still discolored tracks.

"I could kill that son of a - "

She held her finger to his lips.

"Not here, Barak. This is a school."

He stood frozen in front of her. He seemed more like an action guy, but right now, with her fingers against his soft lips, he froze.

His tongue darted out, and he licked her finger. Maybe she would have been weirded out, but the way he did it. The way his tongue did, a slow taste of her skin had her gasping at the fire igniting along every nerve. The damn heat settling between my legs.

"It is a school. I do seem to kind of like these human spawn."

She couldn't help but smile. Regardless of the trauma, the fear, he struck something inside her.

"You like them probably because you think like them."

The way he smiled at her warmed every cold place inside. Every corner that was slowly being frozen by the tendrils of whatever was growing deep in her soul. She didn't dare tell Deo, or worse Barak, that the medications didn't get rid of the strange itch or the ice slowly chasing along her nerves.

It wasn't that she shouldn't. It was that if she said it out loud, it meant it was all real. For the moment, Jenn preferred to tell herself that this was somehow normal.

Except she'd opened the can of worms. The one that confirmed not everything was a hallucination. Probably.

"Want to go somewhere more private?" he asked.

Jenn froze. Did she?

"I. Doesn't it seem a little too soon?"

He blinked, and his lips parted, but he didn't say anything. Before she could ask him more, he gripped her hand as he headed for the door, pulling her to follow.

"Wait. wait." She kicked her room door closed. She was following regardless of what she wanted. Curiosity? Desire to stay near him? She'd figure that out later. "Where are we going?"

He'd never misled her in the short time she'd known him. But this wasn't what she'd expected.

The panic started to set in. A door slammed somewhere behind them. Her chest tightened and air fought to make its way into lungs that seemed to have shuttered up. The visions started. Outlines of figures danced around her. No not danced. Fought? Her body slammed into a hard wall and she blinked.

"Where were you?" asked Barak.

Blinking harder, she wanted to get rid of the vision. A strange electrical current hummed along her skin and she focused against the visions, into the pleasant feel of life. Slowly, white halls and ugly brown and blue titles came into focus again. Focusing on one square tile to another and finally landing on Barak's strange green swirling eyes centered her back in this world.

Her chest pressed against his warm, hardened abdomen. There was nothing she could think about to try and calm herself. Nothing. Except the feel of him helped ground her second by second.

"Calm yourself, Jenn. Breathe in and out. In and out. Here," he said and placed her hand over his heart.

"Feel my heartbeat. Follow it," he said.

She sucked in air and blew it out like there was a race to who could hyperventilate faster.

"I was only taking you to the roof. You said you didn't remember my dragon. I thought that- " he paused.

In out. She repeated the words over and over in her mind.

Jenn stopped and looked at him. "You were just, wait. What? Can you repeat that?"

The look he gave her made her feel like a freak. Except she probably was.

"The roof. I can show you, you aren't nor were you ever crazy."

Her head was nodding regardless of what thoughts ran through. Her body was on some strange autopilot.

Deep breath. Was she truly ready to face the fact she wasn't crazy? Maybe she should want to stay in her fantasy where she could pretend she had just had a nightmare. Maybe.

"How about I carry you up there? If that's okay?"

Jenn reached up and tried to stop herself from the creepy nodding and forced a smile instead.

"Sure." She was ready to see something was real. Something outside of medicine and drugs and the strange lines on her arms that resembled a really bad map of rivers running across the midwest.

His arms reached around her and picked her up. A door

opened up that Jenn didn't even know existed. Hell, there was actually a whole area of the school she swore she'd never seen.

The swift movement of him as he carried her made her feel like she weighed nothing, but in reality, she knew that wasn't true. Well, maybe. She had lost some weight since being rescued. Food just didn't taste the same. Her stomach couldn't seem to remember how to hold a meal down. Hell, she didn't feel the same.

Nothing was the same, and denial couldn't fix that. Life wasn't ever going to be the same and if she didn't stop him right now, he would solidify all that was not right in her new world. If he proved nothing was a hallucination, what was she going to do with the information? The police already had said her case was open. They suspected she was drugged and a part of Jenn wanted to scream that. Yeah, duh. She knew that part.

The gray concrete of the walls to the roof seemed to slow down everything.

Barak was probably moving fast, but she saw it all as an impending change. Her entire world could go from a semblance of a new normal to living in a world where hell not only existed, it was hidden before her eyes.

Crap-cicle. She still couldn't breathe. Her throat was resembling a thin straw as she failed to get enough air.

Barak pushed a door, a ping of something breaking in the process, but her heart's hammering away was all she could focus on. Jenn squinted against the late afternoon sun as they marched out onto the roof.

Did she want him to prove this? Could she still say no?

Could she walk to the edge of this roof and teeter on the edge like her sanity did right this very second?

She was a teacher. She was content with knowledge that had sound logic and, in some cases, hundreds of years of proof.

Her feet touched the ground as Barak shifted her into a standing position.

Taking her hand, she tried to press it against the panicking organ. Her heart.

"Are you okay?" Barak asked.

He held her upper arms still. Probably making sure she didn't fall over.

"Look at me Jenn. Look only at me. Are you okay?"

It took everything in her to force her ears to take in the words and get her brain on board to process the information.

A bird chirped somewhere. Wind brushed through her hair.

"Look at me. Listen to my words. If you aren't ready for this. It's okay. I'll take you home," he said.

More words, she thought. She wasn't okay, but was she ready to know the truth? Yes. She was ready to know that she wasn't crazy. The world was crazy, but she wasn't.

One more glance into his eyes and she realized that she'd trusted him from the very first moment she'd seen him. No matter the form.

"Yes. I think so."

The way his eyes lingered on her face said he saw more than he let on. She hated that for all the fear and confusion in her she not only couldn't hide it, she couldn't help but trust whatever he offered.

The more she stared at him, the more her body calmed from the zombie apocalypse fear state to something around maybe afraid of the dark.

Barak had been coaching her to breathe and somehow she'd subconsciously followed his guide. Sucking in the air and slowly releasing it.

Okay. She was calm. Well, calmer. She was fine.

Her hands caught the wrinkles of her dress. Fudge, was she just rumpled and fragile?

She wasn't going to be turning back her life before the crazy-ass scientist.

"Ready. Let's do this."

God, the way he quirked the side of his mouth made her heart flip its stance on life and swoon. The fact that she was positive her entire world was over and she would never feel anything ever again disappeared. The more she remained by his side, the safer she felt and, strangely enough, this guy had heat shooting down her belly straight between her legs. This world was f-ed up.

He ran his hand over the stubble of his chin and hell. He was sexy.

Sign her up for the mystery prize. She'd take whatever the hell was behind door number one. Or two. Or three. Just let it be him.

"Okay. Stay right there."

He guided her back until her ass rested against a wall.

"Lean there. You sure you're really okay? You truly don't remember me? Well, my dragon?"

Jenn nodded her head. She would betray her nerves if she spoke.

"Perhaps we should tell Deo first?"

He came forward and Jenn stopped him. She grabbed his hands.

"No. I'm good. Please. Show me. Show me I'm not crazy."

For all the nerves making her feel like she could throw up at any second, she truly meant this. She needed this.

"I trusted you then. The day you pulled me from hell. I just can't believe anything from that day. I need you to remind me."

He didn't try to pull away, or maybe she didn't let go. This time, as he approached, she let him come closer and closer. He didn't deny her what she asked, but he seemed to need something else first.

"What did they do to you, my mate?"

Her breathing hitched and she couldn't stop as the intoxicating musk of him invaded her senses. Under his gaze, she already felt naked and raw and beautiful. He made her feel like she was the only woman he'd ever seen and he had no desire to look anywhere else.

"I don't know what they did, but I want to feel normal again-" she broke off. "I want to feel."

His eyes bore into hers. The heat of his body seeped through her dress and chased the cold inside her away. This was what she wanted. To feel the peace he brought her. But, mate?

"What do you mean by mate?" she asked.

There was no humor in his next words and the idea that he believed what he said with so much conviction told her that even without seeing him change into a dragon, this was all real.

"Mate. The other half of my soul. You. I've waited so long for you. I'd believed you didn't exist. Not in this world. Maybe not in a single lifetime."

Those words. All of them she wanted to hear. That even in a strange new reality, she belonged.

"I belong with you?"

He nodded.

"Yes, with me."

His face was so close to hers that she could see every tiny eyelash.

"You're not real, are you?"

He smirked. "I'm very real."

She held her breath as he closed the gap and claimed her lips.

The heat pulsing between them. Tendrils of need burst to life as his lips danced with hers. Real or not, she never wanted this to end. Ever.

Jenn let instinct drive. She wasn't able to trust her own mind anymore. But her body knew what they wanted.

Something hard pressed against her belly and the rest of her body awoke with a hunger that couldn't be real. There was no way that was real. But good lord did her body want her to find out.

Jen started to press closer. Maybe she started climbing him like the mountain he was. She didn't care.

The electric charge as his hands gripped her ass, holding her, elicited a sound she had never made before.

Barak pulled away.

"What? No." Her hands wrapped into his shirt.

The only sound on that roof appeared to be her breathing, and yet he seemed to find her distress funny. It just pissed her off more.

"Why are you laughing, you jerk?"

"You have no idea how much I want to do this with you, here. But, for some strange reason, I feel the sense of decency that you will regret our joining out here. On the roof."

It was then that she looked around.

The walls weren't much up here. There was the small area where they stood, but not much else sheltered her and him. "Oh. But, you were okay shifting up here?"

Her new world now included trying to talk a god of a man into taking her body right here, now.

He shrugged. "Truthfully, I only came up here in case you wanted a ride."

A ride? Oh, did she want a ride. "What kind of ride."

And like some kind of wanton hussy that she wasn't, she reached between them and rubbed at his enormous shaft. "Is this taking me for a ride?"

The blood coursing through her, making her damn body throb with some kind of desperate need, had her acting in a false confidence and damn it if she just didn't care.

6

*G*oddess, even he had his fucking limits.

He blew out a breath as her hand stroked his solid shaft that pressed against the god-awful pants he'd worn to look businesslike. Whatever the hell that had meant. He wasn't hiding anything in them, that was for damn sure. That being said, he would not make any hasty decisions that ended up being mistakes. Probably. Fuck. If she kept that up though, he was going to go cross-eyed in restraint.

Why had he stopped this? She wanted him. The air smelled of her desire, and damn. The way she was holding onto his shaft right now? Yeah, why had he stopped her again?

Ah, right? The first hundred warnings from not only his brothers, but their mates. He didn't trust his brothers much, but their women? Yeah. They seemed to have known what was up. They also were trying to teach him what not to do. He snorted, they were all idiots and had all gotten a mate in some of the strangest ways possible. Key word though? They had all gotten mates.

Fuck. His dick twitched at the attention.

Maybe he should just let instinct drive?

No. He was going to listen to reason.

Her pulse jumped as he wrapped his hand around her wrist.

He was going to listen right after he kissed her one more time. He sniffed at her skin. He needed her to calm down or he wasn't enduring this torture much longer.

"Relax, mate. I will share that soon. Later."

Fuck. Her hand started to press harder, giving him just the right amount of pressure.

"If you keep doing that, though," he bit out between clenched teeth.

Her voice was hoarse and clouded with lust as she answered him. "I want this."

Through clenched teeth, he tried to talk sense into her.

"Not here. Let me take you back to your place."

He braced himself with one of his hands against the brick of the doorframe. Fuck. His head said stop, but the need swirling inside him and the throbbing pain growing between his legs said the opposite.

"You're huge," she said.

He smirked and then covered her gorgeous, pouty lips with his own. There was something about a woman admiring him, or rather something about the way she'd said the words. No, not just any woman. Her. His mate.

This wasn't the woman he'd seen the last few days. No. That one was confused and meek and scared. This one? Well, hell. He liked this version.

He pressed his pelvis into her hand harder, not trying to hide what he was offering. If she was this needy how could he tell her no?

Wasn't this what the goddess had designed them to do? Mates? They were to know each other. Love each other each other without question.

They were made for each other.

His mouth trailed down her jaw, down her neck. He pushed

aside the soft fabric on her shoulder, licking the space he would claim with his bite soon.

Her pulse thundered in his own ears.

He slid his hand lower, over her stomach, her body quivered under his touch. Placing his hand over her hip, he started to pull up the fabric of the dress she wore. It was long and bunched in his hand as he grabbed it up, inch by inch, until he finally felt the skin of her thigh.

Sliding his hand over the soft, smooth skin, he stifled a moan from her lips.

This was so much better than the little sneak peek he'd gotten in her bathroom.

He felt for the soft fabric of her panties, tracing the edge of the elastic hugging her inner thigh.

She didn't stop him. Fuck, she was still gripping his dick.

Her hand squeezed him tighter as he lifted the elastic of her panties and slid a digit over the soft skin between her legs.

Her hips thrust into his hand and he adjusted his grip, palming the sweet vee between her legs.

He could feel the dampness, the need slick between her folds, as she pressed harder against him, and this time he didn't listen to reason. His hand back into her underwear, Barak slid two fingers along her already wet slit, finding the sensitive nub hiding beneath her folds.

He pressed against her and stroked her, giving her what she needed. Every little noise escaping her throat pushed him to give her more.

She broke the kiss to heave in air. Her body shuttered against his touch and she let out a little cry before he'd even entered her sweet heat. Barak pulled her into him, holding her up while he sought more. Sought to ready her for him.

His hand glided easily through her folds to her entrance. He pressed his knee against her thigh and helped spread her leg further, allowing him the access he craved.

His fingers played between her legs, giving her a second to find her sense and a moment to tell him to stop.

"Are you sure?" he asked.

"Yes. More."

He thrust his finger in without a second of hesitation and this time she moaned and without his lips as a buffer, he was certain she could be heard on the street level below. He smirked.

"Shh, princess. You don't want to alert everyone what their teacher is begging for."

She whimpered, but bit down on her bottom lip as he stroked her harder.

"Fuck. You are so tight," he whispered against her ear.

He slipped another finger in, finding the special place inside her that made her grow hotter and slicker. The place that had her reaching inside his pants and grabbing for his dick.

He claimed her lips and pushed in a third finger. It didn't take long for him to coax what he wanted from her. Her muscles pulsed around his fingers and she tried to stifle her cry by kissing him harder.

Barak smirked at the way her body responded to him. Riding out the rest of her release, he finally slipped his fingers from under her panties.

He needed more.

"Don't stop. Please," she begged.

Her eyes captured his, and he couldn't look away. Did she know what she asked for?

"If I don't stop, princess, then you will be mine forever with or without your consent."

She nodded between the ragged breaths.

"You make me feel safe. You stop the nightmares. I- "she paused. He watched as her eyes darted over his face. Her mouth forming words, it appeared her brain needed to catch up with her body. "I need you to chase away the nightmares."

Barak wasn't entirely clear about what nightmares she

referred to. Hell, maybe it was a figure of speech. The way she begged him, though, was all he needed. He would do whatever she asked. He couldn't deny her anything. He would never deny her.

"You are mine to protect." He slowly pecked at her lips.

"Mine to worship," he whispered and kissed her cheek.

"Mine to make love to," he breathed against her ear and licked at the lobe.

"Yes. Yours. Yours to protect," she repeated and unzipped his fly.

"Yours to worship," she said as he hooked his hands behind her thighs and lifted. "Yours to do whatever I ask," she breathed out on a breath.

She'd lost her dainty little shoes as he lifted her, and she made good use of her bare feet. As he lifted her, she hooked her heels around the waistband of his pants and pushed them further down his hips. Her fingers pulled at the buttons on the only shirt he owned that looked appropriate for this establishment. He didn't give two fucks, though. She wrapped her legs around him and slid her hands over his abs. The muscles flexed under her touch.

His dick twitched with the feel of the warmth of her core so close.

"Chase my nightmares away, Barak. Give me something else to dream about."

He couldn't help himself. With one hand, he held her. With his other hand, he produced claws to tear away at her underwear, the last barrier between them.

She squealed and then wiggled her hips, pressing the hot, slick flesh between her legs against him.

He was free to claim her, and he was going to claim her over and over. Now and later.

This was just the beginning.

Lifting her, he positioned her over the head of his throbbing dick and slowly lowered her over him.

This time, it was his turn to moan as she stretched around him. He lifted her up and down, slowly in a rhythm until he finally was able to pull her down, sinking himself completely.

"So tight," he said.

Every breath she took was music to his ears. She was so ready, so needy for him.

Pressing her back against the wall, he thrust into her, slowly at first letting her get used to his size. Letting her feel every inch of him as he pulled out and thrust back in.

He waited for her. Waited for her breathing to grow ragged again. Waited for her nails to dig into his shoulders. She was so close. Fuck. He was so close.

The pressure was building in his balls as he started to take her harder and harder. He couldn't slow down as she crashed around him. The muscles between her legs started to pulse around him and he couldn't stop himself. He slammed into her as he kissed away her release. He slammed in once, twice, three times and then right as he started to spill his own release inside her, he reached down to her shoulder and sank his teeth into the soft flesh as he gave her all of him.

Protect her, he would.

He would give her all the pleasure she could handle.

He held her up for a few more minutes as their hearts slowed from a hammering to a dull thump. He licked at the spot he'd just marked and looked up, catching her dazed and sated expression.

"Princess, you okay?"

She nodded, but didn't say anything. Perhaps she couldn't yet.

He smirked. "I did offer to wait."

This time, it was her turn to smirk. "I didn't accept your offer."

A slow laugh bubbled up. "You are full of surprises, aren't you?"

This statement had her casting her eyes away. "Is that a good thing?"

Barak nodded. "Fuck yes. It's amazing."

She winced, and he froze.

"Are you okay?"

Her cheeks flushed pink. "Yes. More than okay. Just, uh. I didn't. I've never. You're huge and I've never had anyone that-"

He froze. "I didn't hurt you, did I?"

In response, she moved her hips a little. Stroking him while still inside her.

"No. Not at all. Just using a muscle that's obviously never had so much pleasure, ever."

He leaned his forehead against hers. "Good. I never want to hurt you. Ever."

Jenn's fingers played at the hair falling against his neck.

"I know."

He breathed out in a breath he hadn't known he was holding.

"I wish I had been the one to save you." Realization had dawned on him recently. The anger and frustration that Deo had been the one to save her ate away at him. She was his.

He resented Deo for being the one presented to her. He'd also relied on his brother to help save her. But he'd wanted to be the one there for her and it killed him he hadn't been. Now, though. He could be there for the rest of her life.

"You are real? Right?" she asked.

He pulled away, her beautiful pink cheeks coming into a focus. He shifted her, and his dick twitched at the new friction. Slowly, he lifted her, slipping himself from inside her. He hated to separate himself from her, but there would be more time. Always more time. She was his.

Both feet firmly on the ground, she fixed her dress, letting it fall down beyond her knees. The sweater she'd worn with it was askew and she grappled with the fabric, but finally got it righted and pulled it on to hide the marks.

It didn't work, not with him, though. He knew what was beneath.

"I am real. This," he reached for her hand and brought it to his bare chest and laid it over his heart. "My heart beats for you."

She sighed.

"And the dragon? You brought me up here for more than just, well."

The dragon within him stirred at the memories.

"Mating? Yes. I brought you up here to see my dragon."

She giggled. "It wasn't a metaphor then?"

Barak racked his brain for the word. Metaphor.

She's referring to your dick.

Damn brothers, always a few too few thoughts away. It did make him chuckle, though.

"You thought I was referring to my male parts as a dragon?"

He grew hard, watching her nibble on her lower lip. The flesh along her neckline flushed and pink, and her eyes turned down to the floor.

Gripping her chin with his fingers, he tilted her eyes back to him. He would not allow her to be embarrassed or turn away from him, ever.

"Well, to answer your question. It was not a metaphor," he said.

With a quick kick of his foot, he removed one shoe and then the other. His pants were already undone, and he finished the job.

Peeking up at her, he expected her to say something, but instead her gaze was just as hungry now as it had been before he'd claimed her. His dick responded as his brain shorted out.

"Should I undress?" she asked. Jenn's need filled the surrounding air.

"I would show you my dragon. The real one. If you let me. And I need to discard these binding clothes before destroying them."

She nodded, but instead of any of this making much sense to him, she was crossing her legs. Her hands sliding down the curves of her stomach. She pressed against the fabric of her dress with her hands.

Was this normal? Probably? He dropped the rest of his clothes and instead of shifting, he let his instincts drive him. He let the need of his dragon, who was ready to fucking pounce on her, take control.

He growled.

"We should take you home."

She blinked and had he not been a dragon shifter with great hearing; he have missed her next words.

"We?"

He stalked towards her.

"Me and that dragon you won't let me introduce you to."

Jenn swore this wasn't who she was, yet she couldn't stop herself.

She wasn't herself.

Or well, yes, she was.

She was the new her. The her that didn't want to wait for anything anymore. The one who discovered life could end before you had a chance to live it. She was the Jenn plagued by nightmares except when he was here.

Hell, she was the Jenn that just realized how amazing it felt to be touched and screwed and holy hell. She felt alive for the first time.

Her pulse jumped at the sound of his growl. Oh, good gravy. He'd growled.

Thank you for the powers to be, she thought.

Her stomach fluttered, and a heat coursed through her. How was this real? Five seconds ago, she was barely able to stand without the help of the wall. Now? Well, she could do more than stand. She was ready to jump into his arms all over again. The soreness between her legs just made her want to feel him pounding into her again.

Oh, yeah. She didn't want soft and sweet. She wanted him to make her feel alive over and over.

His arm wrapped around her waist and she suddenly realized she'd forgotten how to breathe as her lungs started to burn.

"Barak."

She didn't say anything else before he kissed her so hard she practically forgot her name.

Her mouth was still hungry as he pulled away. Her heart sped up as he gripped her hips and turned her.

She shivered at his large hands running up from her ass along her spine to her neck, gently pushing her forward. She warmed from the heat of his chest against her. Shots of desire sprouted where he touched and spiraled around her body. Every new touch gave way like a sprouting burst of fireworks.

"Hold on, princess," he said. His hands ran along her arms and secured her grip on whatever the hell she was leaning over.

The breeze kissed her bare ass at the same time she felt the heat of his rock solid length slide across the skin of her ass. She swallowed a moan. The muscles between her legs clenched in need and want.

One of his hands gripped her hip, his fingers biting in just the right amount to keep her on this side of pain. Her eyes closed as she felt his thickness spreading her, pressing into her, sliding through her sore muscles and she moaned at the delicious feel of him sinking deeper and deeper.

She couldn't breathe, suddenly aware just how big he was. The fullness of him inside her almost made her wonder how she fit him moments ago, but the pleasure eclipsed the worry. He stretched her as far as she could go, as if she was made only for him.

Before she could process it, all her breath hitched as he slammed into her. The slap of his balls against her ass a new sensation to process except then he started to retreat. Jenn tried to hold in every cry, every needy moan by burying her face into her own arm, biting down against the next cry the second he slammed back into her.

With each new thrust, she bit back each new flood of desire. Closing her eyes, Jenn lost herself in Barak. He knew what she wanted even before she'd been able to tell him.

Holy hell, she wanted more and more and he delivered.

New pulses of energy thrummed through her and the memory of her orgasm before swept through her as the same strange coil began to build. Oh, God, yes.

"More," she said, not caring who heard.

He gripped both hips now. He was the only reason she wasn't slamming harder into whatever she leaned over. He spread her legs even wider with a slide of his foot and it was all she needed. A second later, the world disappeared into a static sensation. Every nerve in her body was alive and she could feel everything between her legs, but nothing else around her existed. Only Barak.

She couldn't catch her breath though, even as she came back to the realization. Every sensation was firing harder and stronger, and she wanted more. She wanted him to come for her. She wanted him to use her until she could no longer find the strength to stand, because this was alive. This was amazing.

Who cared if she ever breathed again. He pushed her over that invisible edge of desire and her body burned in release again. Her muscles quivering around him as he slid back in again and this time when she was certain she would die a beautiful death by his dick, he slammed into her once more and she felt him release again. The heat of him spilling into her, filling her.

He shuddered behind her and then as her own body started to calm, so did he.

He leaned over her and kissed her shoulder. Kissed her shoulder blade, the back of her neck, until she turned to him and let him claim her lips.

"You can't be real."

This was what every romance book she'd ever lost herself in bragged about. Her breath shuttered a moment later following one more quake. A reminder of her pleasure seconds before.

He thrust his hips once more and wiggled a bit. "Are you certain I'm not? Because that feels fucking real to me."

He slid away from her, taking his warmth and her new favorite toy.

"Come, princess. I'd prefer to be in the safety of the indoors as night falls."

She shivered, and cold washed over her. Everything about her little escapade eclipsed by a reality that she still couldn't grip.

He stepped towards an open area of the roof and before she could prepare herself or hell, before she could fix her dress and process the wetness between her legs, a massive green dragon stood before her.

He was emerald green, like fresh blades of grass from her childhood home back east. Or maybe it was like the green of the name brand crayons, not those crappy off brand ones always telling you they were teacher choice.

Whatever he was, he was amazing.

And real.

Very, very real.

Did she touch him? She'd just let Barak do more than touch her. But he was human then. And now? Not.

Breathe. She needed to breathe.

He wouldn't hurt her, and the dragons were the one good memory she had of that hellish place. But still. Officially, she wasn't crazy, and she hadn't created dragons to cope. They were not an alternate fantasy to survive her trauma

Slowly, she grabbed up his clothes from the ground.

The dragon grumbled, and she looked up.

"What? You can't just leave this stuff here. That's got to be against policy or maybe littering or something."

Walking over to him, she slowed the last few steps.

"You're still Barak, right?"

He nodded.

"And you don't talk back. Right?"

In a slightly dragon like move, or maybe it was human, she swore he shrugged.

He sucked in the air around her, the huff audible from his gigantic head.

"Are you sniffing me?"

He made a throaty sound that could have been a laugh. If she'd ever heard a dragon laugh, anyway.

"So do I get on?"

Yes.

She paused. Was that one of the nightmares? Would shaking her head make it go away?

No.

This time, she glared at the green monster in front of her.

Can you read my thoughts?

Her eyes widened at the realization.

I can hear what you share. It is not mind reading.

Share? Share?

"I didn't freaking share anything!" she screamed.

He stood a little taller and circled around her, leaving her nowhere to run.

But you did. We are connected now.

Connected. Something strange seemed to fill her and run through her body. A foreign power that made no sense. She was a human. But she felt like something else. Powerful? Strong? Strange, for damn sure.

"Wait, when we? Did you? Is it your? Does it go away?"

The dragon's tail thwomped against the roof as he seemed to be thinking.

You said you were ours? You are our mate. When we mated, I bonded you to me.

Jenn tried to not flinch when a large talon reached for her

shoulder. The dragon sniffed or did something strange and paused.

Do not be afraid of your mate.

My mate? My mate.

She pulled aside the part of her dress he was reaching for and saw a marking. Newly pink healing scars. A bite?

You bit me?

The dragon had the gall to lick his lips.

You never asked what being mine meant. But you agreed.

Her mouth opened, and then she closed it.

Well, crap on a cracker. He wasn't wrong.

Now what? They were in a stalemate, and she wasn't entirely sure what move to make next.

I feel your confusion, but please get on my back. We need to get inside.

The strange dark green of his eyes reminded her of the man only seconds ago who she hungered for.

Blowing out a breath, Jenn put one foot in front of the other. She could do this.

Probably.

Jenn knew she was fine. This was safe. He was real, and she wasn't crazy. Isn't that what all of this was about? Proving that everything she'd seen was real and the strange dreams? Visions? They weren't hallucinations of her mind.

She got her answer. Too bad the feeling flowing through her was slowly being replaced by the tension of knowing. Life couldn't ever be the same again.

One foot in front of the other. That's all she had to do. Move one foot in front of the other. The dragon, Barak, followed her as she came up alongside him.

The scales of his green skin glimmered.

Beautiful, she thought.

Thank you.

She darted a glance back to his large head as her own face heated.

"I forgot that you can hear me."

Was that a smile? It should have been scarier with those long, sharp daggers for teeth she could see lining his mouth.

It was now or never. The palms of her hands ached, and she stopped clenching her fists.

Reaching out seemed like the best way to just dive in.

The sheen of his scales felt much different from she'd expected. Sure, there was a leathery quality, but he was softer. Her body tingled with strange feelings that had little to do with his hide and more to do with the connection she shared with him.

Her world was dark, but right now? He was a temporary high. He was the only light in her shattered soul right now. Dragon or not.

The more she looked at him, though, a whole new issue came about.

"How do I get on you?"

Before she could figure out much more, her world tilted. Her stomach pitched, and she fell into what she was positive was Barak. The strength before her got lost in the riptide of night-mares trying to compete for attention.

A loud screaming deafened her. It wouldn't stop. She tried to turn away as her stomach finally lost the battle against gravity.

Jenn couldn't take it. She released her hold on the one thing that brought her peace and pressed her palms against her head. The pressure of too many things, too many sounds and pictures, trying to rip through her.

She couldn't do this. She couldn't live like this. If Barak couldn't chase this away, she was lost. She couldn't do life like this. None of this was fake. Nothing in her visions was made up. This was from somewhere. It was all something. Visions of dark creatures that held no corporal body, but still somehow scared the shit out of her plagued her dreams, and now she knew they must all be real.

All of it must be real.

Jenn, listen to me. Focus on me.

She did as asked, and the screaming faded. Slowly, it silenced. For now. As the shrieking stopped, a new exhaustion hit.

She couldn't erase the girl, though. She knew what she saw. There was a girl. What if she was real? She was in trouble. She had to be.

Jenn couldn't focus on the vision, though. Every fiber of her being was exhausted. Just as quickly as things had come on, they disappeared and everything went black. Quiet.

Peace.

For everything she wanted to feel, she realized maybe not feeling might be better.

The last thing she felt was the wind in her hair.

It calmed her and she let herself fall into the reprieve of silent blackness.

8

He'd finally seen it. What she'd been hiding, and it was ugly. Demons? Rancid dark creatures, one that Deo had a hard time forgetting, plagued her too. It hurt that her best way of coping was to have his brother around. His dragon sucked in air and held back the fire in his belly.

She'd still chosen him. She'd chosen him to mate her, even if Deo could understand her pain.

The other comfort was, she hadn't told either of them.

Incoming. He shouted to his brothers.

Barak wasn't sure what else to do except take her to his home. Where she'd be safe and maybe someone, Deo, could find a solution.

Or worse. No one could find a solution.

Barak's dragon shook his head as they glided along the air currents. He held his mate delicately in his claw. He couldn't shake the fear she'd felt. Fuck the fear he'd felt through their connection. What the hell had that been? None of the other mates had anything like this.

He was angry too. No matter how calming flying free above

this alien word should have been, he couldn't shake his anger. This was done to her. She hadn't asked for it.

It was clear this had all started after coming home. This wasn't her power, or not one she had known about.

With a peek down at her limp body, he allowed himself to calm at the sight of her breathing, but her mind was blank. He was happy he could be here for her now. Their mating hadn't been at all what he'd expected, but after this flash of what she was hiding, he would never regret giving into her need.

He had wanted to be the mate to do everything right. What was right, though? Who knew? This had been the right choice for her, or she may not have told him in time. He may not have been here to help her. He could be there for her now.

Relief flooded him. He'd been there to catch her and soothe her. He'd like to think his presence had helped chase away whatever that was. The cry of the woman didn't settle well within him, though.

Brother, what is it? answered Nyke.

Finally.

I am bringing back my mate. She is suffering and I need your help.

Too many voices started in at once. Kal first and then Deo, and they continued. Questions and congrats all flooding him. He could feel their worry. Feel their relief. It was all bitter sweet, and they all mirrored all the feelings he had bottled up in the last few minutes.

His belly burned, but not from dragon fire. No. Anger. That fucking monster had gotten to them again. Tortured another mate. He was so tired of this world and the evil it somehow supported. What kind of planet was this?

The hell that inhabited the surface of Earth needed to come to an end. But only once he figured out how to save his mate.

The connection between them sizzled strong. Her heart beat strong.

Nowhere in any of their training or books could he have truly understood what this connection would be. He could feel it through himself as if she were part of him. Well, she was. She was part of him; she was his soul.

His dragon dipped closer to the surface. They were close to his brothers and together they could solve anything. They'd saved Maddie and Lilly. They'd helped Aisha and Irene. Jenn would be the next mate on their list. The goddess didn't play fairly. Fine. If he needed to go through this to find his eternal happiness, then he would. She stirred in his claws, but the threat of their connection wasn't what he'd hoped.

Dreams? At least she didn't have those visions right now.

Hang on, princess.

She didn't hear him, not consciously anyway.

He'd had her for a whole few minutes before he finally solved the mystery of what plagued her, better than the last week of guess work. Why hadn't she told him?

He'd finally seen where she went when her eyes glazed over. Deo would be intrigued and happy. Him? He couldn't stop his blood from thundering in his ears. The muscles of his dragon's jaw ached. Hell, he hadn't realized how tense he'd been until he was way too far in the sky. Panic had seized him at first. Had he hurt his mate? Consciously, he had to adjust his grip to make sure his beautiful, perfect mate could breathe. He'd sworn he would protect her, but not only had he been lost in his anger, he literally couldn't fight something in her head.

Fuck. I need your help; he said to his brothers.

He needed so much help. He wouldn't survive without her. This was his one in a million. It hadn't been long ago that he'd been with Cy. Losing the hope that this trip had brought. Billions upon trillions of stars and solar systems and they were to find their mates, finally, on this one singular planet. It was the design and yet? They had nearly failed.

Barak felt the ache in his soul evaporate the moment he'd laid eyes on his princess. His mate. Even if she had been confused and drugged. He'd known her the moment he'd seen her.

The ache shooting across his chest now a reminder just how much he wouldn't survive without her. One thing wasn't planned, the visions were driving her mad.

The grass smashed down under his massive clawed feet. They were here, finally. He'd brought her home. Barak gently settled his mate on the soft grass of their new hiding spot while he shifted. Mid step, he walked from one form to the next and gently scooped her back up. Out of the trees came his brothers.

All five of them. The joy that should have been on everyone's face was absent. He gritted his teeth. This was the last time this monster would do this. Barak swore to no one but himself.

"Brother? Bring her inside."

She barely moved as he cradled her against his chest. She was alive, though, and he couldn't sense any fear. Exhaustion? How had he missed how tired she was? Looking down at her as he moved closer to the ship, he noticed the dark circles under her eyes. Not the same look that she had sported when he'd rescued her.

He ducked under a rocky ledge and moved to the other side of the gray expanse. The ship came into view. The new spot served them well enough. Hard to reach by foot being locked on an outcropping with a large enough clearing to get the ship in and out. A few wolves perked to attention, but for the most part they, he and his brothers, were the apex predator and they had no intention of hurting anyone.

One by one, they filed into the ship and he held her closer. Something filtered through to him. She was indeed dreaming, but none of the images made sense alone. One had to be in that lab. Another was how she saw him. And next was a string of strange images. Not entirely different from the vision from before, but this one was strange. Where he'd heard the scream of a woman before, he suddenly had several images of a woman now. What was his Jenn seeing? What were these images?

"Put her here, brother."

Barak hadn't noticed them enter the infirmary. The one room well used in this ship since encountering this asshole of a doctor, or whatever he really was.

Nyke was already pulling over equipment while Deo prepped a needle.

"No. Step away. You are not poking her," said Aisha.

Aisha grabbed the needle from Deo while Irene came up alongside his mate, followed by Lilly and Maddie.

"This isn't just any magic," Irene started to say.

"But Deo and I have been tending to her and it had been helping," Barak interjected.

The four women rolled their eyes. Okay, fine.

"Obviously it isn't helping and Deo said you saw something in her mind. Leave this up to us ladies, boys," said Maddie.

Irene laid her hands on Jenn and he fought his instinct to stop her. But they all knew what Irene could do. What she had done for Eadric.

"This is my father's handy work. I wasn't able to do much that first night, but maybe there's something else? Aisha has been working on a potion to neutralize demonic energies based on Lilly's blood. And mine actually. Mine is a little off thanks to pregnancy," said Irene.

The connection between all my brothers and I was strong enough to feel the joy from Eadric. To feel the joy from many of my mated brothers and one by one, each of their mates would soon carry our young. I couldn't share in that joy, though. I couldn't feel what they felt. Hope.

Everyone was silent for what felt like an eternity. Nothing went fast as he watched her pale features. Irene's hand gently rubbed over Jenn's arms, similar to how she had that first night. Aisha came around and pushed Deo out of the way.

"She doesn't have to drink this. It's a topical potion. While Irene tries to coax out any poisons, I'm going to run this over her skin. Around her temples and along the base of her skull. This isn't science, or well not entirely."

Barak nodded and helped turn Jenn's head. It wasn't that he didn't trust them; it was that he couldn't let go of the need to protect her.

"Please, just help her," he pleaded.

The door opened behind them and he realized Cy had left. It was fine. Barak couldn't blame him. It had been Barak and Cy these last few long weeks. And now Barak was sitting here watching his mate suffer.

All the waiting in the world and it didn't guarantee that the goddess' design would work.

"Whatever my father gave to her isn't a poison, not from the standpoint of demonic energy. Whatever it is, I can feel the presence, but it's become part of her," Irene said.

Everyone's focus was on Aisha now.

"Her pulse is stronger and her coloring is better. Maybe this is working?"

Barak said nothing. He just watched Jenn.

Come back to me. We will fight your demons together.

There was no answer.

"Her vitals are strong. She appears to just be sleeping," said Eadric, watching a machine. Barak nodded.

"Indeed, she sleeps, but what I fear is what happens when she dreams?" he asked. The images in her mind were still confused. What he was noticing though? Is that every few images ended with her looking at him. She always came back to him.

Slowly, noises came into focus. Something moved. Metal grated against metal. Odd creaks she couldn't place. Her eyelids weighed too much. There was something different though, she wasn't drenched in sweat. She wasn't waking in a state of panic.

Maybe she'd lost her ability to function? She moved her fingers, rubbing them against soft sheets or fabric.

Strange new scents told her she wasn't home. Beneath the scents of metal and forest, she could pick out one familiar smell and her heart fluttered.

She could do this. Open her eyes. That was all she needed to do.

Mate?

There was no reason to jump this time. His voice was the deep baritone that pulled her from her nightmare.

Maybe he couldn't keep them away entirely, but he seemed to help her overcome the darkness.

Barak? I can't move.

He grabbed her hand and held it. Sparks enwrapped her skin and up her arm. Strength.

You can. You're just tired. Your visions take a lot of energy from you.

Did they? She'd been tired since getting free and she was positive it was because of what the doctor had done. Only, what had he really done?

"Is she awake?" asked a female voice.

What the hell? Her eyes flew open, and she looked up into the green eyes of her dragon man, but she darted past him to find the female.

A moment ago she couldn't open her eyelids, but now? Oh hell, no.

"Who is that, Barak?"

He smirked, and she took the reserves of her adrenaline to punch him.

Who is that? Are you some kind of dumb species that have multiple mates? Did I just escape one monster - She was cut off from her rant as Barak claimed her lips. He tasted like spiced cider and something else and home.

He was home. She couldn't stop herself from betraying the worry that had replaced confusion.

The way he kissed her made her feel like she was the only woman in his life. Maybe she could just… nope.

As she pulled away from him, she raised her hand to hit his arm, but his reflexes were faster.

Calm yourself. She is not my mate. There is only you and ever will be you.

The curly haired woman peeked around Barak.

"Oh good. You're awake. I thought you were awake. Now we can talk."

Jenn looked between her and then the man, not Deo or Barak, and she breathed.

No. Wait, she could kind of remember this one. Orange eyes? There had been an orange dragon on that building not too long ago and the women seemed familiar too.

Oh. She remembered this one. Slowly, the room came into focus and she saw the others. All of them. One was new, though. She didn't remember one of them. But the rest? They weren't dreams, and they weren't part of her nightmares.

"You were all there when Deo saved me? Right?"

She needed them to all say yes. Confirm everything she already knew. Why did it matter? It mattered because slowly her brain was wrapping around all of it. She was embracing it all. She was. Mostly.

Something tugged at her heart and she went to rub at her chest, only to realize it wasn't her pain. It was Barak's?

This mind reading thing wasn't intuitive and there didn't seem to be instructions coming. Just a crash course. Her mate had more experience and seemed to have locked down whatever he was thinking.

Deo? Was it Deo that bothered him? He'd seemed perfectly comfortable with him, but when she'd mentioned... oh.

Well, there was little she could do right now. She squeezed his hand and tried to broadcast how she felt about her, well what was he. He said mate. That's probably true. But was it like a husband? Answers started to come to her from the group, and she forgot her own questions with the knowledge that she wasn't crazy.

"We were. You don't remember us?" Aisha asked.

"Yes, all of us were there. We did somewhat wonder if you were able to see all the creatures surrounding you," said Maddie.

"Demons. They were demons," she corrected every curious face.

Jenn shook her head. The churning of her stomach and the tightness within her chest and the sharp pain of nails digging into her hand where she squeezed her empty hand into a fist said she wasn't entirely sold, that she wasn't still hallucinating all this.

Barak stroked her back.

They are all real. Just as I am.

"I'm Irene."

Jenn looked at the woman. She was definitely not in the first group she'd met and from the looks of things she was with the guy with the crazy purple eyes. All the guys were vastly different, and from the one very warped memory, they all shifted into a rainbow of dragons.

"Uh. Hi."

Irene smiled, and oddly, Jenn felt better. Not because Irene's smile was beautiful or welcoming. But something in the way of a connection seemed to flow all around her.

Jenn didn't have a family to care about if she disappeared. She'd aged out of the system years ago and fought her way to get a degree in teaching. She didn't want any other child to ever feel like she had.

Barak's hand came to rest on her shoulder.

I am sorry you have no family, my mate.

She closed her eyes for a second, forgetting that he could read her mind. She'd now given him her darkest secret. Her vulnerability.

Only here the loneliness stopped at the door. It could be having this man inside her soul and her head. But that wasn't it. Not all of it, anyway.

"Why does it feel like I know you all? I mean, I know Deo saved me. I know him well. And obviously Barak." She paused at the sting of pain and this time it was obvious it was coming from Barak. She sighed. That would need to be addressed later. Around the room, she settled on another of the females. She needed to figure out who was who and who was with who. "Which one are you?"

"Maddie. And this is Aisha and Lilly," said Maddie. She paused and looked at the other men. Another male came in through the doors. She hadn't realized there was one missing. He stepped forward, but he kept his space. It was hard to miss the fact he had no woman near him.

"Which one are you?" asked Jenn.

He nodded. "Cy. And the connection you seem to feel is the connection between all of us. We are blood brothers. Sworn to protect together. Our mates are not connected the same, but you will know your family. It is the way the goddess wanted it."

Jenn nodded like a bobble head. So many things. Cy stared at her for what might have been too long and Barak held her tighter.

He stepped away, but stayed within the room that seemed much too small for these males.

"Which one do you belong to, Irene?" asked Jenn.

Irene smiled and reached back.

Right. That one.

"This big guy is Nyke. I like to think that he belongs to me, not the other way around."

Everyone laughed, except Jenn. But she couldn't stifle the smile. This wasn't what she'd expected. Granted, what had she expected?

She'd been terrified and the fever of those injections had made her hallucinate beyond just the creatures. Seeing was believing. Only her brain still had to catch up.

Yes. Dragons. Got it. That was real. Her would-be rescuers were all real. That evil man? Had to be real, and she had the marks to prove it.

She swallowed. She wasn't admitting that. Not yet.

"And you?" She pointed to Maddie.

Maddie shrugged and grabbed for the one who had nearly orange irises. "This guy is Kal. Oddly, he's quiet right now. Don't worry, he'll annoy you later."

Chuckles continued around the room and he looked at Maddie with a pure love she was certain each couple had in common.

Jenn snorted. "Do you always talk to him like that? Aren't you worried about making him angry? He is a dragon."

She stopped herself when a look of horror, or maybe it was a strange amusement, passed over their faces.

We could never hurt our soulmates, Jenn. I thought this was understood.

Barak's voice warmed her, and she realized that she believed that hook, line, and sinker.

"Sorry. That was a dumb question."

Irene reached for her hand. "Don't apologize. Most of us have had some rocky starts. Ask all the questions. We are family. Like it or not. I hope you like it though."

Something flashed over Irene's face. Jenn wasn't entirely sure that she'd seen it right, but even as Irene laid down her hand, she was certain they could all communicate around her without her hearing them.

"What? I saw that look. What is it?"

It had taken her a few minutes to realize that she was in a hospital bed, or well, some kind of medical room and the company in here was most likely not for introductions.

"How are you feeling?" asked Deo. He had been the only other person she trusted. Or was it dragon? She didn't pull away. She allowed him access to whatever he needed because he'd saved her.

Barak hadn't left her either. His presence may have been the difference to her calm.

"I mean, I just found out that dragons exist. Or rather, confirmed they exist. Which means that all the things swirling in my head exist. So I mean. I'm living my best life, I guess?"

Deo cracked a smile, something that Jenn didn't realize was a thing.

"Is it funny that I went from feeling a little crazy and now I not only know I am not crazy, but that everything I thought I knew is wrong? And not only that, there is evil in this world I can't prepare kids for. I can't teach them how to battle a demon. Or how to- "

Well crap. She'd said it. She'd said demon like it was a matter of fact. Holding out on this one thing was now over and reality didn't exist as it just had.

"I can't protect a kid from this. I can't even protect myself." That last word was barely above a whisper.

She pressed her hand against her chest. Her breathing was coming rapidly now and forcing the air in and out of her too tight throat was starting to dry it out. The heat of Barak's touch wasn't helping as much as it had a few minutes ago.

Calm yourself, mate.

She couldn't, though. She couldn't calm herself.

She looked over at him as he hooked his finger under her chin.

See me. There is nothing out there to hurt you. I am here.

Energy passed from him to her and the electrical pulse flowing from his palm seeped through her shirt before she realized he was now pressing his hand against her chest. Only his magic, if that's what it was called, actually helped.

"Very good, Jenn," Deo said, like he was some kind of coach.

She could do this. It was all going to be okay.

"Now, Jenn. Tell me. What are these nightmares Barak reported you having?" asked Deo.

What was she supposed to say? That they started out as night terrors the first few days and progressed into debilitating glimpses into what she assumed was psychosis of some sort.

Now? She believed that not only were they not just nightmares, they were something entirely different.

"I think they are visions. Only, I think they are happening now. Not the future."

The room went silent, and the girl named Irene came closer and Deo moved out of the way.

"What are the visions? Barak mentioned something about a girl?"

Irene reached for her wrist, and Jenn let her take it. Barak would keep her heart calm. She didn't need to keep her hand pressing against her chest. Nothing was more help than Barak.

"Yes. The first few nightmares were just the demons. They are always in a dark place, but they have strange energy signatures? Like waves. I don't know if that even makes sense. But I can see them as they move around the space."

Irene nodded. So Jenn continued.

"Well, just in the last day I've started seeing this girl? Well, not seeing. Hearing her. Like sometimes I get a strange glimpse of her. But for the most part, it's always hearing her. I think she's in real trouble." Jenn swallowed. "I think she's connected to me. Or rather, whatever that doctor did, I am connected to her."

$\mathcal{I}$f there was ever a shit show, it would be this fucking moment.

"What the hell. You have all fought for your mates. We learned using them for bait was a shit idea."

Five sets of eyes look back at him. They could fuck themselves.

"We are this close Barak. The plan is coming together. She can help find this missing piece."

He glared. Fuck them.

"I think we all know by now that it isn't our plan that we need to trust or adhere to. Where are they?"

His brothers and Barak had been relegated to the common room for the last hour. Why? Something about girl bonding time.

"I find this ridiculous. We are sitting here for what? I've only had my mate for hours. She's just gone back to work. I would rather go enjoy being with her."

Cy got up and stormed out.

"Fuck. I wasn't thinking."

Kal shook his head. "It's okay. I'll go talk to him. Communications tell me that all is peaceful in the universe, for now. But the elders expect us to get back once this little problem is fixed here on earth. The issue is that Cy still is without his mate. He is feeling the pressure."

Barak nodded, as did the rest of the brothers. They knew that Cy was suffering. He'd been there for each of them. Been there watching as one by one each of them found who and what they needed. Where was his mate, and why hadn't they been able to find her?

"Thanks Kal. Let me know if you think we need anything for him. Perhaps another scouting run? We still haven't seen the good doctor move, but we are also nowhere near knowing how to end him either."

Our elephant in the room didn't have a solution yet, and this plan was meant to find one. Somehow everything we thought we knew was to end with this mystery sister and Jenn was the first we'd heard of a mystery female.

"When have we ever run into such a problem?" asked Deo.

All of us shrugged. I sat down, bracing my hands on my knees.

"Perhaps we should do something the women want to do? For once," said Eadric.

Barak ran a hand down his face.

"Fine. Tell me. What do they want to do?"

Perhaps it had been far too long since their females had been allowed out. Maybe they had been too restrictive, and maybe it was why things were starting to seem dark.

"My mate has been requesting dinner and dancing. Maddie put the idea of some kind of club in her head," said Nyke.

Everyone of them groaned. Kal had relayed what this club was, and they'd all been avoiding it. This might have been selfish, though. Cy needed more chances to meet his mate, and the females needed to find their last days on Earth as memorable.

"I will need to check with Jenn. I believe tomorrow is what she calls the weekend, so perhaps this is a good opportunity."

Barak headed towards the hall but paused as the five females walked in the room giggling and laughing.

Even Jenn seemed to have found her humor and Barak would do anything to keep her in this mood.

"We have a plan boys."

That should have driven fear into all their hearts. Lucky for them, they were ready whether the females knew it or not.

"Please tell us, mates. What can we do for you?" Barak said,

Something that Barak had noticed is that each of the females had somehow found their spot in this strange little family. Cooking had become a group thing for everyone and the males? Well, none of them resented their job in the bedroom. Now, though. The dynamics were clear about who was in charge and where everyone fit.

"Well, we have lots of things to go over. But first things first. We need to discuss how there seems to be a strange coincidence that we each have a strange ability to do things," said Maddie.

Kal came in at that moment. "What are you beautiful creatures planning now?"

Maddie turned on him. "Planning now? Ha. When aren't we planning? Just because we don't include you doesn't mean that we have suddenly started to listen to you. We will never sit down silently."

A smirk spread over Barak's face as he watched Jenn look at him and mouth. Sorry.

"Tell us, oh ring leader. What is the news?" Kal said, leaning in to kiss his mate.

Nyke went over and picked up his mate. She didn't seem to mind being removed from the group.

Come here mate.

The way she smiled at him, he didn't need to feel the relief flowing through her. It wasn't just relief at being near him again, but something new.

Not that he didn't still struggle when looking at Deo. Barak still struggled with the jealousy that his mate viewed Deo as her savior. And fine. He was. But he still struggled with her visions of his brother.

Things had shifted among everyone. Shifted with him and his mate, and none were a threat to him. So he needed to let this shit go. There was more chatter to distract him from his self hatred at least.

Maddie eyed each and everyone of them. "Well, Irene had a theory that somehow the goddess not only brought you here to find us, but something bigger. To bring us together to destroy her father."

Jenn fit into Barak's embrace as they listened.

Aisha smiled as she took over, waving something around. "We played around with the strengths of everyone on paper. We have Maddie, who can absorb powers as well as cast spells. Her forte, though, appears to be absorption. Lilly has demon fire. We are rather positive on this matter. I am a healer or well good with magical potions and tonics that can heal. I think this speaks volumes for my purpose. Irene controls demon energies. We haven't had much time to test this, but we've all seen what she can do. And now, her." Aisha motioned to Jenn.

Barak looked down. "What does she have to do with any of this?"

The females shrugged until Lilly spoke up. "Jenn is the latest in my father's genetic experiments and it doesn't make it okay. But the way this power has manifested, we think that the goddess intervened and gave her the gift of premonition and vision. Some things that perhaps could happen and some things that are. We need to see if she can identify the difference and if she can pinpoint where our sister is."

Jenn, is this true?

She looked up. He would have gone to the ends of the earth to find her, but he also wasn't willing to let her risk her sanity for them or anyone. Would pushing her ruin, Jenn?

"This sister? She is who you think Jenn is seeing?"

The females shared looks and none made him feel warm and fuzzy.

"Answer me, I want to know."

More looks. Fine, he'd try something else. "Do you think that this sister is the key to getting rid of your father?"

No one said anything for a long pause. Irene, however, started to nod. "We think that together we might have every piece to find a way to get rid of him. If anything was learned from this last run in, is that he isn't human. Not any more. We won't be getting rid of him by any standard means."

Barak held onto Jenn.

"Standard means? Have we tried to contact whatever fucking organization he partnered with since burning him out hasn't worked for shit?"

Why did this feel like talking to a wall?

"My father went against the Illuminati years ago. They would have eradicated him had they had the means. Jenn has the ability to see things for a reason, and she should lead us to what we need," Irene said.

"Why do I feel like there is a but coming?" He asked,

Maddie shrugged. "Because you know as well as any of us do that in order to do any of this there will be some kind of crappy cost and although we want her to learn to be calm, we need her to control the visions to give us what we need."

If things got any more cryptic, Barak was going to scream.

"So what is the plan, then?"

Jenn turned around.

"They want to see what happens to me in a more stressful environment. Somewhere loud and obnoxious."

Eadric started to laugh.

"This is an elaborate way of trying to get us to go out, isn't it?"

All the females gasped. "What? Never."

And one by one, their cheeks turned rosy as their mates caught on and probably did what he was about to do.

Mate. Are you lying?

She shook her head rather aggressively.

Liar.

I looked at my brothers and in seconds each snatched up their mate and had them over a shoulder. Jenn squealed as I picked her up.

Meet back in an hour to take them out, broadcast Deo to everyone of us as each male took his mate to their quarters.

"Put me down Barak. I promise. We just want to test what I can do."

The door swooshed closed behind them. The room was familiar to him, but he enjoyed the new addition way more. There was no denying the way his groin throbbed as he watched her breasts bounce when her back hit his bed.

"Mate, how dumb do I look? We were not born yesterday."

Jenn squirmed up on the bed.

"No one said you were. I swear they said they just wanted to go out and see if different stresses triggered me."

Barak climbed up onto the bed after her. "They played you, princess. They have been trying to find a way out of this ship from the first day we locked them in. All we want is your safety." He paused. "You knew that, though. Your heart betrays you."

He watched her lips press together. He didn't have to know her mind to know she was caught in his trap.

"I didn't know that. Not entirely."

Barak enjoyed seeing her squirm. He took in the clothes she wore.

"Is this a borrowed outfit? One of the other females felt it would better suit the mission?"

The soft leather of the skirt felt like butter under his touch as his hands slid up her thighs.

He passed up the tiny black thing and traced her thigh.

Her skin dimpled at his touch.

Do I make you nervous?

She made a little squeak, and then her head lolled against the pillow behind her.

No. Maybe. What are you doing?

He licked his lips. *What any male would do to a mate that thinks she can trick him.*

Her breath hitched, and the air scented of not just the sweet scent of her need, but something else.

"Are you angry?"

She shook her head. "No. But, I mean. What are you going to do?"

He pushed her skirt up and pushed her knees apart. A growl escaped his lips at the sight of her bare with no panties to stop him from taking what he wanted.

"They didn't have any new underwear, and I didn't want to wear someone else's..." she broke off as his lips started to kiss a trail up her thigh.

I like this look.You should do this more often.

His tongue watered at the idea of tasting her. He was getting so close to the sweet center of her body and he could envision what it would be like to make her squirm.

He ran a slow lick up her slit, slowly spreading her with his index finger and letting her feel his intentions.

Shall we see if this situation triggers anything? He teased.

It didn't take long for her to respond to him; her folds becoming slicker and the scent of arousal becoming stronger than her nervous energy.

"What are you doing?" she asked between pants.

Punishing you for lying to me.

The air hissed through her half open mouth as he slid a finger inside her and he pressed his tongue along her sensitive nub to stroke her. He worked her on the inside and on the outside. He used his free hand to hold her thighs apart, keeping the control in his court.

Her fingers wrapped in his hair, driving him to push her harder and faster.

When her breathing became short pants and her mind a jumbled mess of cries, he knew she was close.

He stroked her harder and faster and slid in another finger and then a third until he was certain she'd not only come for him, but that she would want more.

Jenn shattered around him, and he lapped up her release.

She was his and his alone. He'd have to teach her that there were consequences for thinking she could play with him and she would enjoy every second of it.

*O*h hell.

"Barak, what - the - oh - God-" she couldn't finish one damn thought.

Don't talk unless it's confessing, he taunted.

She wrapped her hands in her hair." Oh, God," she screamed.

He pulled his fingers away and he gave her a second to catch her breath. Her entire body was hot. Her toes tingled with the reverberation of her release.

"I might lie more," she said and immediately regretted it.

He yanked up the hem of her shirt and licked at her exposed breasts through her lacy bra. Oh, good heavens. She was going to die. She could feel it. Her soul was definitely leaving her body.

Barak started to climb up her body. His hard body brushed against her skin, her peaked nipples. He dipped his head and kissed her, igniting the same fire inside her all over again. The difference was, she'd let him have control before and now it was her turn.

Something pulled at the back of her mind. What if this was all some kind of dream, even if she didn't want it to be?

She wanted to remember everything about Barak for as long as this would all last.

She pushed her palms against his hard pecs and he rolled them, but he wasn't releasing her lips and she was okay with that.

My turn, she thought.

Holding herself together as she rubbed her slick heat against his solid and ready shaft was almost too much for her. He moaned against her mouth. The power of being in control of this magnificent man felt empowering, though, and she was determined to make him come for her before she would come for him again.

She broke the kiss this time and smirked. His eyes were glossy from his own need. Her body burned, and she realized she could feel his want within her and it burned so brightly she wasn't sure she wouldn't come again the second he entered her.

She slid him between her slick folds, rubbing her sensitive clit against him until she couldn't hold in her own cries of desire.

Aligning herself over him, she slid him inside her, slowly. Inch by inch, memorizing each ridge of his silky shaft. She relished the burn of her stretching muscles until he was fully seated within her and she moaned at the feel of him filling her.

Maybe she didn't know what she was doing, but her body did. Moving her hips, she rocked against him. The ridges of his abs under her touch contracted.

The threads of their connection lit up in electric need with every single undulation of her hips.

Everything felt more. There was nothing else to describe her high as she ran her hands along his stomach and over the planes of his body. She closed her eyes and let herself feel. Jenn memorized the feel of him inside of her as she used him to chase away the last few weeks. To push away the demons.

She pushed herself over and over until the sweet vibrations of her impending orgasm started to hum and the world fell away.

She lost herself between the line of almost there and almost too much. Breathing no longer mattered. The sweet spot between her legs riding the edge of pleasure and pain. This was real.

She chased the pleasure until she couldn't stop it, and she exploded around Barak. Her core pulling from him.

Before she could slow and ride him until the end of her own rapture, he wrapped his arm around her and flipped her over.

Hold on, princess.

And hold on, she did. Her hands shook with her tight grip on his forearms as he took her for a ride, slamming into her over and over. He pushed her own senses to build again and just when she was positive she couldn't breathe, that her body was coiled too tight, he slammed into her one more time and shuddered on top of her. She let her body release once more, not that she had any choice. He was perfect. Her body hungered for him, and it reveled in the joy that her pleasure only added to his own.

She moaned at his kisses. He shifted and her sore and still quaking core welcomed the feel of him pulsing inside her.

"All this because we wanted to go out?" she asked between breaths.

He laughed, still atop of her, and she squirmed under him.

"No. That was just a bonus. We were planning to take you all out anyway and used this as an excuse to get ready. Perhaps we put back on this little outfit I enjoyed so much?"

She nodded, knowing that she would have been happy never leaving his bed.

Our bed, princess. Ours.

A smile slid over her lips. Was this all real?

Don't leave me. She clung to him like he was a solid tree in gale force winds.

He nodded and pulled her in tighter.

Jenn hadn't gone out to any place like this, ever. She'd been human and this? This wasn't human.

She'd been excited until she wasn't.

Barak? I was kidnapped outside of a restaurant. Please don't leave me.

This was much busier than any restaurant and yet no one had noticed her disappear there. Here?

Barak had agreed to this. Why? Oh right. They all had agreed to go out. Was it too easy? Jenn thought so. She had expected Barak to fight it a little. All the other girls said their dragons were fiercely protective and although Barak seemed the same, he'd still allowed her to come with.

It was for a purpose. Irene had suggested seeing what environments triggered the visions. Chaos? Calm? Panic? Irene hadn't mentioned panic, that was all Jenn.

Jenn tended to think the visions were anywhere Barak wasn't. She hadn't yet slept, though, so to think the night terrors were gone would be premature.

For now, she would go along with this plan. So many questions filled her, though. The girls had said they would all be leaving soon? What did that mean? Could she still teach? Were they leaving? Did dragons all live in strange ships? She didn't dare ask if it was a spaceship. She'd just now embraced demons and scientists that were villains from nightmares. What next?

Princess, breathe. Yes, spaceship. I can hear your thoughts clearly. Calm yourself. This is fun.

She looked up, and he did exactly what she didn't know she needed. He kissed her. She would be okay. She would.

You will be okay. Barak tightened his grip.

She would be fine.

The group headed through the club and Jenn had yet to feel a pull to the strange place, her nightmare world. No hot flashes of the otherworld come to get her.

A strange electric charge seemed to spark though, and Jenn

assumed it was simply the energy of the club. Bodies filled the space and as they moved through crowds, Jenn could feel the room closing in on her. Her stomach soured. Each new ragged breath tasted like stale beer.

Calm. It's okay.

Okay? No. It was not okay. The hands grabbing for her reminded her of that last night in the warehouse. Too many things reaching for her. Touching, grabbing. She was certain they were here. She couldn't have a vision because they were all already here.

She jumped as something rubbed her ankle.

Relax. It was just a skirt.

A skirt? Hell no it wasn't, except as she tried to look back and she didn't see anything inky black. No creatures with razor teeth or tentacles instead of arms. Nothing but bodies of humans.

I will never let anything harm you.

She tried to turn to see him, but she tripped. Barak caught her, and she realized that she wanted to know what would happen if he ever didn't catch her?

She scratched at her arms again. Here, no one thought much of the strange lines that had only started to fade. They still remained like dry creek beds, an ever-present reminder of what once was. She couldn't forget.

Her feet remained on autopilot, following the group. At least it wasn't hard to find the dragons. Even in their human forms, they were a head taller than the tallest human and built like football players. Their wide shoulders made it easy to squeeze in the wake of the bodies that moved to allow them to make their way.

Still, it was too many people.

"Barak?"

He looked down, but helped her continue to navigate the crowded place.

What, princess?

Barak, can we go outside?

He didn't need to say anything. He just nodded and helped her change course in the room.

She appreciated his size and the fact people naturally seemed to sense the strength, or perhaps danger. Jenn trusted her mate. That took a lot to process. Mate. That was like more than just a word. Maybe it was more than just the human word for husband?

At least obsessing about this made her forget, sort of, the fear of being here in a place where something could hide and grab her.

She'd been taken from somewhere she should have been safe. But would she ever be safe? Safety at home? Even that wasn't real. It was just an illusion. These things could get into anywhere and anything.

Barak loosened his grip as he pushed open the door and they stepped out into the night.

The driveway, or perhaps alley, was clean and quiet. Dark. But quiet. There were a few people sprinkled about smoking. It didn't stop Jenn from jumping every time a shadow moved as the person attached to its image shifted.

"Jenn, calm yourself. This is meant to be fun. We know you all had a plan to test what triggers you, but it was also meant to help release stress."

Jenn turned around and hugged him.

"Thank you."

The electrical charge made her shiver. It wasn't going away.

"Of course. I want nothing more than for my mate to be happy. I would also like to know how to help you."

She shrugged. "I think I am beyond help. Or maybe I just need time. I do know your strength helps."

The feel of his hands rubbing up and down her back brought comfort, and replaced the tickle that something was off. No, not replaced, just dulled it.

"Maybe we should get Deo?"

The words left her mouth before she could remember the tension from earlier.

"Why? He can not keep you safe. He has his own mate."

The edge of Barak's voice told her that it was exactly the wrong thing to have said.

"That's not what I meant- "

She couldn't finish her thought, let alone her words. His lips crushed hers. The wind ripped around them before she realized her feet were no longer on the ground. His hands were everywhere.

"Stop asking for my brother," he said, pulling his lips away.

She swallowed. "I didn't. I mean, he helped me."

Wrong thing to say.

He slammed her back against a wall, buffering the pressure with his arms. His mouth consumed hers and she was lost for a few seconds.

My brother was in the right place and at the right time. He isn't your mate.

She blinked as he let her breath.

"I know. He just - "

She trailed off as he pressed the massive bulge in his pants against her. The skirt rose up as she shifted.

Don't say his name.

"Okay." What had he asked?

She couldn't remember anything except the feel of his tongue against her skin.

I am your mate; he said.

She wanted his hands to go lower.

Yes. My mate.

Jenn didn't care what he said right now, as long as he kept doing that thing to her ear.

"Can I trust that this is closed?"

She blinked. "What? Is what closed?"

Oh, good gravy, he was still kneading her breast.

"Better. Should we go back?"

Her attention came back into hyper focus.

"What? No. You can't start molesting me and then just flip a switch. I can tell you aren't ready to go back. I'm not going back, unless you want to confirm with Deo about what-" she said.

She would have been proud of herself, except that she couldn't remember why as Barak lifted her. Heat flooded between her legs as she felt him shift beneath her, and before she could figure out how he'd unzipped his pants, he was thrusting into her.

She gasped as he stretched her. She moaned as he thrust into her again and again.

It wasn't sweet or romantic. It was animalistic, and she wanted more.

I am your mate.

Jenn might have said yes. She might have just puffed out air. She couldn't be positive of anything.

His thrusts were powerful and relentless. Her body taking everything he had. She couldn't stop herself from screaming his name out loud. She couldn't stop herself from screaming. He kept pushing her and her body did whatever he asked. She came for him in a powerful wave and her entire body came alive with every sensation she'd never known she couldn't feel.

"Oh, God."

Barak slammed into her again. He needed something, and she would give him everything.

The goddess can't help you, he thought.

Her hands dug into his shirt, twisting into the fabric, praying she didn't fall to pieces as she crashed into one orgasm after another. The sound of him taking her as he spread her wider with one hand while the other braced her against the wall faded away into the static vortex of motions that was her world.

"Yes, Mate. You're my mate." She barely got the words out as she crashed into another frenzy. Her body struggling to know up from down or left from right.

The muscles inside her core pulled and stroked him and begged him to come with her. Finally, after her lungs burned in protest at her lack of breathing, his dick pulsed inside her. He claimed her lips and rode out his release as she fought her own. Slowly, his body calmed down.

The anger leaching through their connection slowed.

"I am your mate. You never ask Deo, or anyone, anything. I am here for you."

He could win this argument, because right now she couldn't remember her own name. She couldn't remember how to walk.

"I am yours," was all she said.

"Let's head back?"

Barak couldn't release her, not yet, regardless of his words. His senses were tingling and although he should have been relaxed, the air was feeling less and less promising.

He smelled her hair because nothing was better than the scent of his mate.

"I know you just smelled me."

He adjusted his hold around her as she breathed deeply.

"And you just did the same."

He knew she smiled even without seeing her.

Maybe he'd let his jealousy get to him, but at the same time, he didn't want to change a thing. She was relaxed now, unlike earlier where she'd been so wound up he'd been waiting for her to burst into tears or, hell, bolt for the door. Either wasn't what his brothers or himself had been trying for.

While she relaxed into him and he tried to ignore the nagging deep within his gut, he half shifted and slowly brought them back to the street. His wings retreated back into their metaphorical state in his soul.

She was fine. She would be fine. Only, he wasn't entirely sure that was true. He paused. Those weren't his thoughts, and this nagging wasn't really his eyes.

Princess, you keep saying you will be fine. Are you not?

She snarled at him. "Stop it. Get out of my head." She pushed him away.

He watched her scratch at her skin and, as much as he wanted to respect her, he couldn't stay out of her head. He needed to know how to fix her. Fix this.

She couldn't block out the itch of the insistent currents of something strange in the air and he noticed her scratching faster and more fiercely. Something was wrong.

"I won't be fine. I can't figure out how to forget. It haunts me. I won't be fine."

The two other people that had been in the alley moments before he'd taken her up to the roof were gone and they were alone.

"I can't forget. It's everywhere. I can't forget."

Barak reached for her. He tried to wrap his arms around her, but she wouldn't let him.

"Stop. Stop it. You're calm and comfortable and God, everything good in my life. Don't come closer right now. I can't have you become part of this."

The pain flowing through her had him lost. His hands felt empty and he couldn't stand still. He needed to hold her. Make it all better. She just kept backing away. What could he do with himself to help?

He'd reach for her and then pull his hand back. He'd step back trying to give her space, but that didn't feel right either. He rubbed at his chest with the confusion of who's pain he felt. His own? She was falling apart and he couldn't do anything to stop it.

Something was wrong, and it was swallowing her.

"Stay away. It hurts, Barak."

He took a step forward, and she didn't notice.

"What hurts?" he asked.

She rubbed harder and harder. Even in the darkness the red of her skin was obvious.

"Stop, Jenn. Please. There is nothing there. Nothing to rub away."

"It burns. Something burns. I can't breathe."

Calm, mate, he thought.

She glared at him. "If I could calm, I would. This isn't a panic attack. It's something else. Something new."

He tried to come for her again, and she backed away.

Her voice filled his head as she took a step after step back.

Please, let me keep you safe.

Barak's head snapped up as a strange energy whipped around him. Maybe not him, but the air sparked and flickered with energy signatures so similar to Irene's own strange kidnapping. He would never forget that night like all the others in their time here.

"Jenn, please come back to me," he called.

"Don't you feel that?" she cried out.

Barak looked around. "I do. Please come here."

She snarled. "The power? It's everywhere. Something's coming. I can't be here. I can't be here for it."

Her body turned toward him, and he was certain she was coming back. Before her feet could find perch and propel her to him, something flashed before her and grabbed out into the night.

Barak lunged at the purple field of strange magic seconds later as the last finger of his mate disappeared and the portal with it.

What the hell?

He couldn't stop himself from projecting his fears to everyone. This was the same as Irene. She'd been swallowed by hundreds and thousands of demons. This? There had been nothing but energy.

He turned in a circle, sniffed the air, and came up with traces of things he'd never smelled before.

Demon magic, like the doctor? Maybe? His mate, though, her scent was gone. Just vanished.

What the fuck had just happened?

What happened, Barak? called Deo.

Barak looked up and down the alley. What had happened?

The door swung open with a burst of sound and music and heat. His brothers strode out, ready for something. An attack? Probably. All their mates were behind them, but as the realization of the attack hit, everyone fanned out.

"What happened? My mate was here and the next second someone grabbed her and pulled her through what I think couldn't be anything except a portal?"

Everyone glanced around like the fucking thing would still be there. Barak wasn't sure why he wasn't more angry. Why wasn't he more afraid? Shock? Probably.

He could still feel her. Sense her. She wasn't answering, but he could still feel her. She was alive. *I feel her. Whatever took her doesn't know how to block our connections or maybe has no idea they exist?*

Five sets of eyes met his. And four women gathered around each other, talking.

"What are you females going on about?" he asked.

Irene turned to Barak first.

"This is what we were hoping would happen. Maybe. Well, not this. But you know."

This spiked the anger that had moments ago appeared dormant.

"What the fuck are you talking about? No. I do not know."

His brothers created a wall around the females like he would jeopardize anyone's future. His voice was something between a human and his beast a breath later. He now realized he was mid shift. His dragon had surfaced and as he focused on pushing the beast down, that's when it all hit him. All the panic. All the pain.

"She's gone. She's really gone?"

He grasped at the air where the portal was and felt nothing. He stepped further from his brothers and their mates and then allowed his dragon to emerge. They would find no help here, and if Irene and the others had assumed that this would happen, that his mate was expendable, he didn't need them.

One quick look back and he shut out his brothers and thrust himself into the sky. Follow the thread that connected Jenn to him.

If he pushed himself to the edge of his ability, he would find her alive. What he didn't know was why she didn't answer and why she didn't reach out.

This wasn't how this was supposed to go.

He flew in the direction of his heart.

He would find her.

It had been hours, and he was finally getting close.

A portal was the only thing that made sense. No other option existed to get a person halfway around the world this quickly.

He'd crossed water, what earth called oceans, to find her, and here he was drifting over an expanse of forest until he caught something.

His dragon sniffed again. It wasn't a memory and wasn't his mind playing tricks on a desperate man. It was her. The wind called him to her and he obliged.

Slowly, he allowed himself to drift down into a large enough clearing his dragon could fit easily. The sun still wasn't peeking over the horizon, but he knew morning wasn't far off. He needed the element of surprise.

Barak sniffed at the air again. Jenn, yes. Trees, yes. Something else? The forest was a mix of too many things to pick out anything.

Jenn didn't seem to be panicked. There was that.

Princess, I am coming.

There still didn't seem to be anything.

He was confused and shifted quickly. The trees made it hard for his dragon to seek around, but in human form he still took the ground as quickly as he could manage to track her scent. It wasn't a clear path, rather the wind would ebb and flow and calm in a rhythm that made it harder and harder to lock onto her. What kind of trickery was this?

A glinting light made itself visible the closer he got to the scent of his mate. A soft voice spoke, and he strained to hear it.

"Dragon. I sense you out there. Come closer."

Don't go in without us.

Barak scowled but remained silent. He didn't need them. They'd been more than happy to put his mate into a test he didn't agree on.

*J*enn blinked at the flickering of a fire. Her mouth tasted like ass. Or well, maybe cooked cauliflower. It wasn't good. Her shoulder hurt as she shifted and something jabbed her in the ribs.

"Dragon, I won't harm you. Come to me."

Jenn shot straight up and brushed away the twigs making her shitty bed.

"No. Don't. Don't listen to her."

Too late. Barak's massive shadow stepped out into the clearing that she was stuck in. Stuck? Maybe not. Jenn wiggled her ankles and moved her arms.

"Jenn? Right? You've been watching me for sometime."

Jenn shook her head and squinted into the dimness.

"It's about time you woke up. I didn't realize the portal would knock you out like that. Strange creature you are. Not typical of my father's creatures. You're much, plainer?"

Jenn wrinkled her nose. "You're plain."

The girl laughed, and Jenn shrunk back. Yeah. She was by far one of the more beautiful women Jenn had ever seen. That sucked. It sucked worse as the woman took in Barak's naked body.

"Hey. That's mine. Stop looking at him."

The woman smirked. "I don't think you get to choose a man like this? He does the choosing from what I can tell."

Jenn went to say something, but realized it didn't matter.

"What are you doing with my mate?" Barak asked.

The girl took them both in. "Interesting. Mate? That's fair. I still stand by my projection that you did the choosing and not the other way around. Strange that you picked her."

Jenn pushed her way to her feet and took a step forward.

Barak nearly flew to keep her upright as she stumbled.

"Interesting. You feel a connection to a creature of my father's?"

Jenn glared at Barak.

What is she babbling about?

Barak shrugged.

"Father? You're a creation of the doctor we have been plagued by?" asked Barak.

The girl swirled her hand in a circle and up popped images, one of which was Dr. Rollings, the evil insect of a man.

"Yes. Only I don't remember this sister. I've been trying to find them for years and this one, she called to me," said the girl.

Barak looked between the two.

"She isn't your sister. Not by birth. Dr. Rollings only recently tampered with her DNA recently," answered Barak.

The girl shook her head.

"Oh, goody. A new one." The woman cackled, and it sent shivers down Jenn's spine.

Barak shifted his stance between them. This girl seemed a little more on the insane side of things.

"You'll excuse me. My father's antics do not amuse me. I've been living to escape him for so long and I finally think I've found the keys to ridding myself of him and no. I get something, or rather a sister that is new and well, you look rather useless."

Jenn sidestepped Barak and balled her fists. Her feet much more cooperative, now.

"Oh, calm yourself girl."

Jenn snarled. "I have a name. It's Jenn. And I am not useless. I've been able to watch you. You should be lucky that your dad doesn't still have me."

The girl nodded and looked back at Barak.

"I suppose she does have some use. You are quite a big guy, aren't you? Are there more of you? I've seen images in her head, a purple dragon perhaps? Some of her memories are very spotty when she dreams, but she dreams of many of you."

Oh, God. That wasn't going to settle Barak one bit to know she dreamed of all the dragons. Wait, did she? Hell, she wasn't sure that was even true.

"Barak, I swear I-"

"Oh, stop weird human hybrid thing. Not like that. You stalk me when you sleep and I've been able to sort of invade those dreams at times to see the images. I need to find the yellow one. I don't know why. But I need him. Is there a yellow one?"

Jenn's heart calmed a little. Oh, she could set her up with a yellow dragon. That wasn't her dragon.

"What do you want - "

Jenn put her hand on Barak's chest.

"Sure. Maybe there is. You want to come home with us?"

Can you hear me? she asked Barak without turning to see him.

Of course. You were much too quiet earlier. It scared me.

She kept her face stony serious.

I have a feeling that she wants Irene and Lilly.

Jenn tilted her head as she watched the girl in front of them lose her stony exterior and falter as she took a step forward.

"Yes. If you can find me the yellow dragon."

She fell to her knees and Jenn ran to her.

"Are you hurt?"

Jenn's hand came away a deep red.

"Oh no. You're hurt. I'll protect you. I'll get you to him. I promise."

Barak came up next to them both and held Jenn.

"Do you understand any of this?"

She nodded.

Yes. Take us home. We can't stay here.

As the words left her mouth, the trees swayed and Barak did what Barak and any other dragon does well. He shifted and circled around Jenn and the girl.

The girl was shaking as Jenn helped her onto Barak's back.

So much blood was all she could see as the night lit up into an orange blaze.

Hurry. There are too many of them.

Jenn grabbed the hand the girl gave her and Barak took off into the sky, but not before something burned around her ankle. Still, she made it onto Barak's back and the bonfire in the forest faded into the brightening sky.

EPILOGUE

CY

*S*omething wasn't right. But then again, what had been right from the start? Now he sat in the commons with the women trying out something they called TikTok looks.

"Holy hell, Cy. Do you have any idea how hot you look?"

He growled. "What does that even mean?"

Maddie whistled, and he glared.

"I need to get out there and do something," he snarled.

Lilly shrugged. "You can't. You're stuck watching us while everyone else paces." She glanced towards the doorway, just as he had over and over.

"Barak is an idiot," he said as something was traced under his eye.

"Seriously, what's this that you are doing to me?"

Aisha moved to sitting on the table. "You do realize that we're bored and none of those idiots will sit down long enough to entertain us. So this is your fault."

"Blink, Cy."

He did as one of the females instructed and felt something sticky on his eyelashes.

"This is what I get for being kind to you females? I should never have taken pity on you creatures."

They giggled, and Cy tried to be mad. At least he was useful to the females. His brother's had followed Barak as far as the shore, before realizing they couldn't leave their females unguarded. Cy tried to swallow the jealousy. At least being unmated meant he, on the other hand, was ready to follow Barak just to realize his brother didn't want him either. The shift in Barak's attitude wasn't good.

Now Cy not only didn't have a mate to be useful for the future of the species, he now wasn't wanted by his brother.

Little did he realize that to be of use to the mates of his brothers he would be put through some kind of makeover hell.

Finally, one of the females held up a mirror.

"What do you think?" Maddie asked.

His eyes grew wide.

"What the hell is this?" he asked, trying to figure out where on his own face he could touch.

"It's hot. You were hot before, but you have the bone structure to pull off this makeup," Maddie continued.

Irene smiled, and Cy hated the glint in her eyes. "You're that guy that would look super sexy with a few piercings and tattoos. Well, beyond the marks of your dragons."

He glanced down at the swirling lines of his dragon marks as she called them. His were along his forearms and they glowed a little more brightly as his dragon woke up.

He stirred, and something within Cy sprang to life.

Brothers, we need help. Cy, she asked for you.

Cy story is next in DesperatelySeekingDragon!

Space Dragons Seek Mates
Book 1: Must Love Dragons
Book 2: Single Red Dragon
Book 2.5 Dragons Under the Mistletoe
Book 3: Dragon Wanted
Book 4: Looking for a Good Dragon
Book 5: No Scales Needed
COMING SOON!
Book 6: Desperately Seeking Dragon